"There's always a catch." Kalissa smiled.

Riley agreed with that. "Catch is—" he settled a hand on her bare hip "—I'm falling for you."

Her smile widened. "That's not a catch."

It was for him, and that was the hard truth. He was quickly coming to care for this woman, but he was destined to upset and disappoint her. There was no way around it.

But not now, he told himself, not today. They could be together for a little longer yet, before the real world crowded in.

* * *

Seduced by the CEO is part of the Chicago Sons series: Men who work hard, love harder and live with their fathers' legacies...

Dear Reader,

Welcome to book two of the Chicago Sons series, stories of betrayal, conspiracy and long-lost secrets.

In *Seduced by the CEO*, the past and present collide when Riley Ellis falls for his estranged half brother's new bride. But then he discovers a family secret: Kalissa Smith isn't his sister-in-law at all, but her long-lost identical twin. Locked in a fierce battle with his brother's company, Riley looks for ways to use this to his advantage.

Kalissa suspects Riley is too good to be real, but the astonishing truth is beyond her imagination. She's made the mistake of falling for him while he's used her as a tool for revenge. Too late, Riley realizes he's the one who's made the mistake in letting Kalissa get away.

I hope you enjoy the new installment in Chicago Sons.

Barbara

SEDUCED BY THE CEO

BARBARA DUNLOP

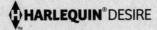

Recycling programs
for this product may
not exist in your area.

ISBN-13: 978-0-373-73395-8

Seduced by the CEO

Copyright © 2015 by Barbara Dunlop

Printed in U.S.A.

www.Harlequin.com

Barbara Dunlop writes romantic stories while curled up in a log cabin in Canada's far north, where bears outnumber people and it snows six months of the year. Fortunately she has a brawny husband and two teenage children to haul firewood and clear the driveway while she sips cocoa and muses about her upcoming chapters. Barbara loves to hear from readers. You can contact her through her website, barbaradunlop.com.

Books by Barbara Dunlop

HARLEQUIN DESIRE

An After-Hours Affair
A Golden Betrayal
A Conflict of Interest
The Missing Heir

Colorado Cattle Barons

A Cowboy Comes Home
A Cowboy in Manhattan
An Intimate Bargain
Millionaire in a Stetson
A Cowboy's Temptation
The Last Cowboy Standing

Chicago Sons

Sex, Lies and the CEO
Seduced by the CEO

Visit the Author Profile page at Harlequin.com, or barbaradunlop.com, for more titles!

For my husband

One

Kalissa Smith stripped off a pair of dirt-streaked garden gloves and paced backward from the Newbergs' house, smiling with both pride and satisfaction. It had taken a full month, but the new lawn gleamed emerald under the August sun. Beyond its scalloped edges, fresh, black dirt was mounded in flower beds positioned against the brick walls of the two-story colonial. Evergreens and dwarf maples were clustered in one corner of the spacious yard, providing shade and privacy.

"The ornamental peppers definitely work," said Megan, crossing from their company pickup truck in the driveway.

"It's a bit of a twist," said Kalissa.

Megan drew a deep breath. "I think they'll be happy with the twist."

"They'd better be happy."

The Newbergs were not the easiest clients in the world, but at least the job was finally complete.

"Did we make any money on this one?" Megan asked.

"I sure hope we did. We were underwater on the turf, but we saved on labor."

"Only because we did most of it ourselves."

"Good thing we charge ourselves such reasonable prices."

Megan smiled at the joke. "It does look fantastic."

Kalissa couldn't help flexing her sore shoulders. Her calves were tight and her abs ached from so many days of physical work. On the bright side, she had absolutely no need to visit a gym, and she was developing a very nice tan.

"I'm going to take some pictures for the web site," she said.

Mosaic Landscaping had been in business for just under a year, starting when Kalissa and Megan had both earned college diplomas in landscape design.

"There were three more inquires on our voice mail this afternoon," said Megan.

"Can we at least grab dinner before we start a new project?"

Megan chuckled. "On top of everything else, you want *food*?"

"Call me high-maintenance."

"I could go for a burger."

"Benny's, here we come."

Benny's Burgers was a funky little restaurant tucked in an alleyway near their landscape shop on the west side of Chicago. They'd rented the aging storefront and warehouse space because of its generous size and reasonable rent. Esthetics had little to do with the decision—though they had painted and brightened the upstairs apartment, moving two single beds and some used furniture into the space.

Kalissa retrieved the camera from the front of their serviceable, blue pickup truck, making her way around the yard to take shots from various angles.

At the same time, Megan gathered up the last of the hand tools, stowing them in the pickup box. Then she perched herself on the tailgate, scrolling through pages on her tablet.

"Any new inquiries from the web site?" Kalissa called as she lined up for a picture of the flagstone walkway edged with pink and white peonies. The front porch and double doors filled in the background, and the sun was hitting the flowers at just the right angle.

"There are still a lot of people looking for maintenance."

Megan and Kalissa had talked about adding a yard maintenance service to their business. It wasn't where they wanted to focus, but if they could hire a decent crew, they might be able to make a little extra money. Their business was gradually increasing its customer base, but the margins were thin.

Kalissa clicked the final shots.

"What do you think about doing that?" she asked as she made her way back to the truck.

"Is there something you've neglected to tell me?" Megan was staring at the tablet screen.

Kalissa stopped in front of her. "About what?"

Megan turned the tablet so it was facing Kalissa.

Kalissa reached out to steady it.

She squinted against the bright sunshine, and a photo of a bride and groom came into focus. The man was handsome in his tux, and the woman's dress was gorgeous, highlighted by a huge, multi-colored bouquet of roses, tulips and lavender.

"See it?" asked Megan.

"The Ferdinand Pichard roses?" They were stunning. Kalissa had never seen them in such a deep magenta.

"The *bride*."

"What about the—" Then Kalissa saw it. She snapped her hand back in astonishment.

"It's you."

"It's not *me*." Kalissa peered at the woman's startlingly familiar face. It obviously couldn't be her.

"Photo-shopped?" she asked.

"That's what I thought," said Megan. "But there are a bunch more." She moved so they could both see the screen while she scrolled through other pictures.

"What on earth?" Kalissa took control of the tablet. "Is this a joke?" She looked at Megan. "Did you do this?"

Megan stood up for a better view. "I only found it two minutes ago."

Kalissa stopped on a picture of the bride and groom cutting the wedding cake.

"Nice," said Megan. "Seven tiers."

"I obviously have money in this alternate life." Kalissa took in each of the bride's poses and expressions. "Too bad I can't float us a loan."

She struggled to figure out where her head shots could have originated, guessing this was some kind of on-line game.

"My birthday's coming up," she ventured, trying to imagine who, other than Megan, would spend this much time on a joke gift.

"Nice groom," said Megan.

Kalissa took another look at the man. "He is pretty hot."

"It says here he's Shane Colborn."

"Why do I know that name?"

"Colborn Aerospace," said Megan, identifying a prominent Chicago company.

"So, it was obviously somebody from Chicago who did this."

"I mean, this is the real guy. He *owns* Colborn Aerospace."

"Uh, oh." Now Kalissa was worried. "He's not going to think this is funny. Can anybody see this page?"

"I got it from a Nighttime News link."

Kalissa's confusion grew. "The national site?"

Megan nodded.

"Why? How? We have to get them to take it down."

"I think it's legit."

"That's ridiculous."

"I think you have a doppelganger."

"That's not a real thing." Kalissa studied the bride's face. "And there's no way someone could possibly look this similar."

It was a joke. These had to be pictures of her that somebody had taken without her knowledge.

"Maybe you were part of a cloning experiment?"

"I doubt they had human cloning when I was born."

"I hope they still don't have it now," said Megan. "You know, there is one other possibility."

Kalissa waited a moment. But when Megan didn't finish, she glanced up. "What?"

"You have an identical twin," said Megan.

Kalissa shook her head.

"You *were* adopted."

"I was nearly a year old when I was adopted. My mother would have known if I had a twin sister. She would have said something."

Gilda Smith hadn't been the most organized person in the world. She was fond of sherry, and her memory was never the greatest. But you didn't forget that your adopted daughter had a twin sister.

Megan looked pointedly down at the screen. "Maybe they split you up."

"Who would do that? And why keep it a secret?"

"It says she's Darci Rivers. Well, Darci Colborn now."

"My birth name was Thorp."

"And your legal name is Smith. Whoever adopted this Darci would have changed hers too."

"It can't be," said Kalissa, fighting the logic of Megan's assumption. "It just can't."

Megan shrugged her shoulders, clearly resting her case.

As Kalissa took in every inch of the woman's face, her chest tightened, and a strange buzzing sensation made its way along her limbs. She struggled to wrap her head around the information.

The resemblance was far too close to be a coincidence. Unless this was some elaborate photo-cropping joke, there was a real possibility she had a secret twin sister.

"You should call her," said Megan. "Maybe *she* can float us a loan."

Kalissa was appalled. "You didn't actually say that."

"The woman just married a billionaire."

"So what?" The Colborn money had absolutely nothing to do with Kalissa.

"The minute she gets a look at you—"

"I'm not about to let her get a look at me."

"Why not?"

"Because I'm not going to be that person."

"Really? What person is it you're not going to be?"

"The long-lost relative who pops up the minute there's money in play."

"You don't have to ask her for money."

Kalissa wasn't fooling around here. "It doesn't matter if I ask or not. They'll think I've been waiting in the wings all these years, and now I've decided to pounce."

"She'll probably just offer it up."

"*Stop* it."

"We'd pay her back."

"See?" said Kalissa. "*See?* Even you think I'm after her money. And you know me better than anyone."

"It's not like she'd miss a few thousand. *Temporarily.*"

Kalissa closed the window and handed back the tablet.
"No. No. And no."

"You can't just ignore this."

"Watch me."

Riley Ellis was both thrilled and terrified. He had a newly
expanded aircraft factory, a significant new sales contract, a
massive mortgage on the commercial building and a maxed
out line of credit. Ellis Aviation was entering a whole new
phase of existence.

"Flipping the switch now," he said to Wade Cormack on
the other end of the cell phone in Seattle.

"Congratulations," said Wade. He was the owner of Zoom
Tac, the company supplying most of the parts for the new
E-22 short haul jet.

Riley twisted the switch, and the main overhead lights
came on in sequence. Computers came to life, and robotic
machines started their power-up sequence along the assembly
line. The hundred staff members on the floor sent up a cheer.

He hadn't really turned everything on with a single switch.
The supervisors and foremen at each station had simply taken
the overhead lights as a signal to go live. It was eight a.m.,
August 16th, day one of the expanded operation.

From the interior walkway on the third level, Riley gave
everyone a wave and a salute. "The clock is officially tick-
ing," he said to Wade.

The cheering gradually died down, and everyone's attention turned to their tasks.

"Now you just need to get the glitches worked out of the
supply chain," said Wade.

"The custom rivets finally arrived. Colorado's good on the
sheet metal. How are your new parts certifications coming?"
Riley moved along the walkway to his office, the spring-
loaded door shutting out the noise behind him.

"My guys say they're on track."

"That's great." Riley plopped down on his desk chair.

The new office was compact and utilitarian, with big windows overlooking the factory floor. His production and sales managers had offices on either side of him, with the various unit supervisors near their staff's stations throughout the facility.

Out of habit from all the recent construction, he'd worn cargo pants and a t-shirt, his feet clad in steel toed boots. Part of him was itching to get down there on the floor and plunge in. But he realized he had to stay at the helm.

He had over a hundred and fifty workers now, operating on three shifts. They needed a leader, not a colleague. And he had to keep focused on the company's strategic direction.

"Good luck," said Wade.

"Talk to you in a few days." Riley ended the call.

As he settled back in his chair, his thoughts went fleetingly to his father, Dalton Colborn. The man had never once acknowledged Riley as his illegitimate son, and he'd certainly never given him any support or encouragement. Still, their lives had ended up following a similar path.

At the moment, Riley couldn't help but wonder if this was how Dalton had felt in the early days when his fledgling company had first started to grow. Had he experienced this same combination of exhilaration and flat-out fear? Dalton had gone from nothing to a billion dollar aerospace company before he'd died, so he must have taken chances along the way.

Shane Colborn had inherited that dynasty. Shane was the legitimate son, the golden child.

"Well, Shane," Riley said out loud to the empty office, wishing he had a shot of tequila or even a beer to use for a toast. "Let's find out if your illegitimate half-brother can give you a run for your money."

His phone pinged with a text message.

He set aside his thoughts and checked it. The text was from Ashton Watson, his high school friend. It was a photo tagged: Blew my mind.

Another text came immediately from Ashton. I've met the bride.

Curious, Riley tapped the photo. It expanded to show a

picture of Shane dressed in a tuxedo standing next to a gorgeous, auburn haired woman in white lace. She had a trim body, bright green eyes and flawless skin, a true ten on the hotness scale. Then again, a ten was exactly what Riley would have expected for Shane.

His office door opened, and Ashton strode right in. "She's a piece of work, that one. Nasty as they come."

"She doesn't look nasty," Riley couldn't help but observe. She looked classy and beautiful, and also very happy. Then again, she'd just married a billionaire in a lavish wedding that was reported to have cost several hundred thousand dollars. That would probably make the nastiest of women happy.

"Just don't tick her off," said Ashton.

"How do you know her?"

"She was Jennifer's roommate."

"Jennifer?"

Ashton gave an exasperated sigh, lowering himself into the single guest chair. "I dated her for four months."

"Did I meet her?"

"Yeah. At least once. I'm sure you met her. Blond hair, blue eyes, great legs."

"You just described every date you've had since freshman year."

"She was different. Anyway, it doesn't matter. It's going to go bad for Shane. I'd put money on it."

"Couldn't happen to a nicer guy," Riley drawled.

Ashton grinned and cocked his head toward the interior windows. "Looks really good out there."

"I can't believe we're finally up and running."

"I knew you'd do it."

"I haven't done it yet." Riley rose to gaze out at the factory himself. Machines were running. People were working. But it was a long, long road to any kind of profitability. He sure hoped he could make it.

Ashton stood beside him. "Yeah, you have. Before long, you'll have more contracts than you'll know what to do with."

"Believe it or not, I've been thinking about Dalton."

"Seriously?"

"I was thinking, he had to have started out like this, same risks, same fears, same hopes."

It took Ashton a second to respond. When he did, his tone was thoughtful. "You're more like him than Shane is, you know."

"That's not my ambition. Riley had no admiration or respect for his biological father. He hated the man."

"Shane had it handed to him on a silver platter. You had to fight for every inch to get where you are."

"Where I am is deep in debt and tip-toeing along a cliff of complete disaster."

"That's what makes it exciting," said Ashton. "No risk, no reward."

"Is that why you fly the way you do? The adrenaline rush?"

Ashton was a helicopter pilot, and he volunteered for search and rescue on his days off. He had a reputation for saying yes to the riskiest of flights.

"Sure," Ashton said with a shrug. "That and it impresses the girls."

"Like you've ever had trouble getting girls." For some reason, Riley took another look at the picture of Shane and his bride.

"Her name is Darci Rivers," said Ashton.

There was something compelling in the woman's emerald eyes, a secret in her lush smile. Riley suddenly pictured her shiny hair splayed across a white pillowcase.

He shifted and quickly banished the image.

"You think he made a mistake?" he asked Ashton.

"Oh, he made a mistake all right. That creature's got claws."

"Well, I hope she distracts him," said Riley.

He and Shane would be going after the same airline contracts from here on in. If Shane was newly married to a handful of a wife, it might give Riley an advantage.

Through the glass of the restaurant window, a good looking, neatly dressed man caught Kalissa's eye for a second time.

He was staring openly now as she wheeled a trio of azalea plants across the lighted patio garden.

It would be nice to think he was interested in her. He was extremely attractive, with dark eyes, a straight nose, and the kind of square chin that made a man seem powerful. But she was dressed in dirt streaked blue jeans, a faded green T-shirt and a pair of scuffed, serviceable work boots.

Her hair was pulled back in a ponytail. At least it had started the day that way. By now, it likely resembled a rat's nest. And the morning's fifteen second application of mascara would have long since rubbed off.

No. The thoughts running through his head were not about getting her phone number. Judging by his growing frown, he was probably offended by her dirty, disheveled state as he tried to enjoy a refined meal.

She kept right on walking, focusing on the uneven cobblestones in front of the wheelbarrow tire, finally stopping at the raised garden bed between two magnolia trees.

"Two foot intervals look right to me," said Megan, straightening from where she'd dug a trio of holes.

Kalissa focused her attention on the garden bed that stretched along the wrought iron fence. "As long as the evergreens stay properly trimmed, this is going to be stunning."

Someday, her budget permitting, Kalissa wouldn't mind dining out here, or even inside. Her gaze darted back to the bank of windows that revealed the elegance of the main dining room.

The man was still staring at her, and she quickly looked away. He was probably just curious about what they were doing—though it had to be obvious. It was also possible he was bored with his dining companion and seeking a distraction.

Despite herself, she covertly shifted her glance to take a look at his date. She was surprised to find he was sitting across from a man. The man looked serious, gesturing with his hands as he spoke. It could be a dull business meeting, she supposed. They were both wearing suits.

"Let's do it," said Megan, releasing the rope on the burlap sheet that surrounded the azalea's root ball.

Kalissa quickly took the other side of the plant, lifting it and then adjusting it to position it in the hole.

Suddenly, a male voice surprised her. "What are you doing out here?"

Megan looked up, and Kalissa turned her head.

It was the man from inside the restaurant, and he was obviously angry. Her first thought was that they had somehow disturbed his dinner. But they weren't making any noise. Surely planting azaleas wasn't that objectionable.

She straightened to face him.

"Are you spying on me?" he demanded.

The question took her completely by surprise. "Am I what?"

"You've been watching me."

"Only because you were watching me."

He gestured to the wheelbarrow and the plants. "What *is* all this?"

"Azaleas," said Megan from behind her.

"We're planting azaleas," said Kalissa, squaring her shoulders and folding her arms across her chest.

He scoffed a sound of disbelief. "Outside my window."

"You *own* the restaurant?" Her question was sarcastic. If he had anything to do with the management of the restaurant, he'd have known Mosaic Landscaping was working here all week.

"I meant the window next to my table."

"I have no idea who you are," said Kalissa. "What's more, I don't care who you are. If you'll excuse us, we have work to finish."

"You have no idea who I am?" There was a note of disbelief in his voice. He jammed his thumb over his shoulder. "And I'll bet you have *no idea* I'm having dinner with Pierre Charron?"

Kalissa reflexively glanced at the window. Then she looked straight into the stranger's eyes. "None whatsoever."

His steel gray eyes narrowed.

"I'm getting the manager," said Megan.

"No, you won't," said the man.

"Excuse me?" said Kalissa, widening her stance. "You think you can stop us from getting the manager?"

"You're bluffing," he told them with conviction. His critical gaze took in her outfit. "You're not going to want to explain this to any manager."

"Explain why we're planting flowers?"

"Explain why you're trespassing."

Kalissa searched her brain for an explanation. He'd accused her of spying. What was he doing worth spying on?

"Are you breaking the law?" Perhaps they'd inadvertently stumbled on something to do with a crime or maybe national security. Should she be frightened?

"I can't believe he sent you." Then a flash of confusion came into the man's eyes. His voice lost some of its edge. "*Why* did he send you? Why *would* he send you?"

Kalissa extracted a business card from her pocket and held it out. "Mosaic Landscaping," she said. "See, that's us."

Looking suspicious, the man took the card and read it.

"Nice level of detail," he said, sounding ever so slightly impressed. "But why you?"

She took a stab at answering the bizarre question. "Because I have a diploma in landscape design."

He drew back. "Are you serious?"

"Completely serious."

He took a long look at her clothes and her hair. "It still doesn't make sense."

"It makes perfect sense, when you think about it," said Kalissa.

Her apprehension began to moderate. The man was clearly more puzzled than angry.

He shook his head. "Why send his wife? He wouldn't send his wife."

"I'm not married," said Kalissa.

"Give me a break."

"Kalissa?" Megan interrupted.

"No, seriously," said Kalissa. She stripped the glove from her left hand and wiggled her fingers to show him.

"The diamond is probably in your safe."

"Kalissa."

"I don't have a safe."

Megan grasped her shoulder from behind, stepping closer. "Kalissa, he thinks you're *Darci*."

Kalissa twisted her neck to look at her friend. "What?"

"She *is* Darci," said the man.

"Darci," Megan repeated with a meaningful stare.

"Darci Colborn?" Kalissa asked, the lightbulb coming on inside her head.

"This is ridiculous," said the man.

Kalissa turned back to him, realizing there was a simple explanation. "I get it. I'm not Darci Colborn. I look a little bit like her."

"A *little bit*?" asked Megan.

"The jig is up," said the man.

"There is no jig, and it's not up. I'm Kalissa Smith. I can prove it. I have identification."

He peered at her, and the minutes stretched by. It was obvious his brain was piecing through the situation.

"What have you got against Darci Colborn?" she asked him.

"I've never even met her."

"Then, that's why you're confused. She's quite different than me in person."

"You know her?" he asked.

"I've seen videos."

"They're twins," said Megan.

"We don't know that," Kalissa said to Megan.

"You should contact her," said Megan.

"Shut up," said Kalissa, having no intention of getting into that debate again, now or in the future.

"This is going to keep happening," said Megan.

"It's a fluke."

"You're a landscape designer?" asked the man.

"Yes."

"Your name is Kalissa Smith."

"Says it right there on the card."

"And you don't know Darci Colborn?"

"Didn't even know she existed until last week. It's weird, but it's no big deal."

"I'm sorry," he said, looking like he probably was, even though he was still watching her intently.

"No problem."

The strength of his gaze sent a shimmer through her chest. He really was an incredibly good looking man. He was tall, fit, and somewhere around thirty. Too bad she was such a mess. And too bad his interest had nothing to do with her personally.

"Can I keep the card?" he asked.

"Do you own a house?" asked Megan, stepping up beside Darci. "Do you have a yard?"

He pocketed the card. "I do. Goodnight, ladies."

"Goodnight," Kalissa automatically echoed.

With a nod, he turned to walk back to the restaurant.

"He was hot," said Megan.

"He was strange," said Kalissa, watching his broad shoulders as the glass door opened and then swung closed behind him.

But she had to admit, he was also hot. There was something extraordinarily sexy in his deep voice. Part of her hoped he might actually call. Against all logic, that same part couldn't help but hope it would be about more than just landscaping.

Two

The next evening, sitting on his deck with Ashton, Riley was still trying to figure out Kalissa Smith.

His brother's wife had a sister. She had a sexy, feisty, *secret* twin sister. And nobody seemed to know she existed.

"Setting aside the 'how on earth' questions," said Ashton, helping himself to a slice of pizza from the carton on the wood slat table between them.

The sun was setting beyond the park, over the vast stretch of orderly rows of houses north west of Chicago. The lengthening shadows showed Riley's yard as plain and stark.

"Setting that aside," he said, though he'd pondered the very question in bed last night, then again at work today.

He'd also pondered Kalissa, her crystal green eyes, those deep red lips, and what looked like a perfect body, nearly but not quite camouflaged by her work clothes. He'd checked social media sites today, but there were no tagged photos of Kalissa Smith. Her name was on the Mosaic Landscaping site, but it didn't have her picture.

"Could she have been spying for her sister?" Ashton asked.

Riley had considered and discarded that theory. "If she was, she deserves an acting award."

"And it seems pretty elaborate," said Ashton, propping his feet up on one of the wooden stools.

Riley had to agree. "There's no way she overheard our conversation from out on the patio. All she could report was that I met with Pierre Charron, and maybe for how long. And why would you use a Darci clone to do that? There are far easier ways. Bribe a waiter, for example."

"So, what are you going to do?"

Riley reached for his cell phone. "I'm thinking about doing some landscaping."

Ashton smiled. "Keep your enemies close?"

Riley fished into his shirt pocket for the Mosaic Landscaping business card. "I don't think she's the enemy. I don't know what the heck this is all about."

"You think they're really twins?"

"They're absolutely identical."

"You sure it wasn't Darci?"

"I'm positive. I checked. Shane and Darci were at an art gallery last night, a charity event on the other side of town."

Ashton was silent for a few minutes. "Then why pursue it? What's in it for you?"

Riley dialed with his thumb. "I don't know yet."

Ashton shifted in his chair, turning sideways to face Riley. "You're attracted to her."

"She's attractive," Riley admitted.

"This isn't about wanting what Shane's already got."

Riley frowned. "I've been over that for a very long time."

"You sure?"

"Yes."

"Mosaic Landscaping," came Kalissa's breathy voice.

"Is this Kalissa?" He already knew the answer.

"Yes, it is." She sounded like she was slightly out of breath.

"This is Riley," he hesitated over his last name. "Have I called at a bad time?"

"Not at all. How can I help you?"

He pictured her pushing a wheelbarrow, flushed cheeks, a bead of sweat at her temple. "I was hoping to make an appointment with you."

"Okay. Are you looking for a site visit? Or do you want to come into the office?"

"The office. Is today a possibility?"

"Um." She blew out a breath. "We'll be back there in about an hour. Is that too late?"

"An hour is fine." He glanced at his watch and realized it was coming up on seven. "Long work day?" he couldn't help but ask.

"About normal," she said. "Riley...?"

"We met last night."

There was silence on the other end.

"You asked me if I had a yard."

"Megan asked you if you had a yard."

"Well, I do. Have a yard." He gazed out over it, knowing the front yard was just as neglected. "I've been thinking about it, and it could use some landscaping."

"Is this a joke?"

"No joke. I need some landscaping."

Ashton rolled his eyes and lifted his beer to take a swallow.

There was another pause before she continued. "What's the lot size?"

"Seventy by one-hundred and thirty. I have an oak tree."

"Bully for you."

"I mean that's all I have. It's a patchy lawn with a single oak tree. It's pathetic, really. I don't know how you'll save it."

"Maybe we should come out and take a look," she suggested.

"I'd rather talk first. You know, toss around some general ideas."

"Whatever you prefer. Seven forty-five? Mr…"

"Seven forty-five sounds good. I'll be there." He disconnected.

"Smooth," said Ashton.

Riley reached for his own beer. "I don't want to tell her my last name."

He didn't want her to know he was Shane's competitor. She might not know the Colborns yet, but Riley was willing to bet she'd meet them soon.

"Make one up," said Ashton.

"I don't want to lie to her either."

"Ha, there's a challenge. She's coming to your house, and you'll have to write her a check."

Riley had already thought of that. "The house is registered to Ellis Aviation's numbered holding company, and I can pay the bill in cash."

"Oh, that will allay her suspicions. She'll think you're a criminal."

"Or a conspiracy theorist." Riley took a thoughtful drink. "You know, that could work. I accused her of being a spy last night. If I behave like I'm generally paranoid, she'll think it's just my personality."

Ashton chuckled. "Can I come along? This sounds entertaining."

Kalissa couldn't decide if Riley was paranoid, a covert operative or maybe even in the witness protection program. He claimed to be a conspiracy theorist, but she wasn't buying it. Never mind that few conspiracy theorists would describe themselves that way, over the past week she'd found his most dominant characteristics to be intelligence and hard work.

He was far more normal and much more agreeable than he'd seemed at first, and she hated to think that somebody that great looking and sexy would be unbalanced. It wouldn't be fair to the women of Chicago.

After thinking it through, she was going with the witness protection program theory.

He'd offered to pay a premium, so they'd bumped him to the top of their list. After some initial work, mostly to level the ground and rip out the sickly lawn, the delivery service had dropped off a load of milled, Colorado flagstone. The installers were due on Thursday to lay the rock for the patio.

She was excited about the patio, and in particular that Riley had agreed to a spa and barbecue area. It was exactly how she'd do the yard if she was the owner. She knew the final photos were going to look great on their web site.

The sun was setting now as she made her way around to the back of his house.

"Thirsty?" Riley surprised her by calling down from the sundeck above her.

She looked toward the sound of his voice.

"Looks good." He nodded to the flat stones piled on wood pallets. Their tones were rich and varied in rust, browns and chalk. "Come on up."

"Sure." She crossed the raw dirt to the outdoor staircase and made her way up to join him.

"Iced tea?" he asked as she made it to the top. He gestured to a pitcher on a round wooden table that was bracketed by two wooden deck chairs.

"Love some."

She lowered herself into one of the chairs, taking the weight off her tired legs.

It had been a hot day, and her powder blue cotton shirt was clinging damply to her body. Her jeans were dusty, and her hair was sticky with sweat and garden dirt.

She pulled out her ponytail and ran a hand through it, discovering a twig and a couple of leaves. She couldn't help but sigh as she discarded them. It seemed Riley was never going to see her at her best.

He'd arrived home from work about an hour ago, just missing Megan who'd left for another jobsite. He was dressed in his suit pants and dress shirt, his tie loosened around his neck. His hair was neat, his face clean shaven, and his fingernails were spotless.

She glanced down at her own fingers and curled them into her palms. She'd worn gloves all day and kept them relatively clean, but she was in desperate need of a manicure. She couldn't remember the last time she'd worn nail polish or had her hair trimmed. She'd pretty much kill for a spa day.

He poured the iced tea. "Looks like you've made good progress."

"Your lawn is gone," she acknowledged.

"Wasn't much of a lawn to start with."

She didn't disagree. "There must have been a lot of annual ryegrass in the mix. Did you aerate, fertilize, re-seed?"

There was humor in his eyes. "Your lips are moving, and sounds are coming out, but…"

She found herself grinning in return. "Never mind. We'll take care of it."

"Where's Megan?"

"We're starting another job over in Oak Park."

"You seem busy."

She accepted a glass filled with sweet tea and plenty of ice-cubes. "We're getting there, slowly. We keep adding casual workers to our roster. But it's hard to be competitive and still make a profit."

"I hear you." He gave a sage nod as he sat down.

"You said you own your own business?" She'd come to understand that he was a private person, but she hoped he'd share a few more details.

"We manufacture parts, mostly for the transportation sector. Margins are tough in any business."

"How long have you been in business?"

"Ten years all told. I started small. You?"

"Just under a year. We've been working hard, and our customer base is gradually growing." She lifted her glass in a toast. "Thank you for adding to it."

"I'll tell my friends about you."

She took a sip.

"Anything you need me to do tonight?" he asked.

Though he rarely got home before seven, Riley had jumped in on several occasions, getting work done after the crews left, both to save money and to make things smoother the next day.

"We've leveled the ground." She rose to gaze over the rail. It was growing dark, but she could still make out the newly worked area in the yard. "Next step is for the installers to lay the stone."

Riley rose and moved to stand beside her. "Next step requires professional expertise?"

"It does."

"And I'm not an expert."

"Not unless there's something you're not telling me." She let the comment dangle, wondering if he'd decide to divulge something new.

A gust of a breeze came up, and she brushed her loose hair out of her face.

"There is something I'm not telling you," he said in an oblique tone than triggered a shimmer of sexual awareness.

"What is it?" She found herself holding her breath.

The silence stretched, so she looked up. He was closer than she'd realized. His gaze was warm and intimate.

The awareness increased, warming the surface of her skin while paradoxically raising goose bumps.

Without a word, he brushed a stray lock of hair back from her temple.

His callused fingertips seemed to hum against her skin. His touch felt good. It felt sexy.

"You're incredibly beautiful," he whispered, easing slightly closer.

The statement took her by surprise. "I'm mostly dusty."

He smiled. "I can't see any dust. But I can see your gorgeous eyes, and I can see your beautiful lips."

His smile disappeared, and he ran the pad of his thumb across her lower lip.

"Soft," he whispered, leaning in.

She drew in a breath and held it.

His palm slipped up, cradling her cheek, his fingertips easing into her hair. He bent his head.

She stilled, waiting.

The kiss started soft, but soon heated between them. Her fingers curled into her palms, and she stretched up. Her lips parted, and he firmed his own, bracing his free hand across the small of her back.

She opened wider, and his tongue flicked in. She met him with her own, angling her head. She raised her palms to his chest, sweeping them upward, marveling at the definition of his pecs, then the breadth and strength of his shoulders. Her arms wound themselves around his neck.

He pressed their bodies together, her breasts against his chest, his thighs hard against hers. The kiss was sexy and deep, oddly familiar. She wanted more from him, even as she acknowledged this was happening at lightning speed.

He seemed to sense her hesitation.

He broke the kiss, drawing back.

"Wow," she managed.

"Wow," he echoed, gazing into her eyes.

The sun was completely gone now, and soft darkness surrounded them, a shaft of yellow light coming from a small window in his house.

He kept his arm around her, still holding her close. "You should come out with me."

She hesitated, unsettled by the sudden shift between them. "I don't usually…"

"Kiss like that?"

"Date customers." Though she had to admit, she couldn't remember a kiss like that.

"You've only been in business a year," he said. "It can't have come up that often."

"I suppose," she was forced to agree.

"Has it ever come up?" he asked.

"Not really."

"So you don't have a rule against it."

"I don't have a rule for it either."

"Where do you want to go?" he asked.

She cocked her head. "I haven't said yes."

"I figure I'll increase my odds of a yes if you like where we're going."

The logic made her smile. "Take a stab."

He smoothed her hair again. "No help from the lady?"

She struggled not to react to the intimate touch. "No help."

"Navy Pier. Ferris wheel and a pretzel dog."

She was surprised, but also intrigued. "You're inviting me out for a *pretzel dog*?"

"I'll throw in some ice cream."

She put a note of astonishment in her voice. "You expect me to say yes to that?"

He didn't look worried. "You don't strike me as a symphony and Le Petit Soleil kind of girl."

She wrinkled her nose and gave a little sniff. "That's only because you've never seen me clean. It's an unfair bias if you ask me, and not worthy of you, Riley."

Uncertainty finally appeared in his eyes. "You'd prefer the symphony?"

She'd liked teasing him. "Your first instinct was right. Add the fireworks, and you've got yourself a deal."

He gave her a squeeze. "You're messin' with me."

"I am."

"I shouldn't like it so much."

"Probably not."

"Can I kiss you again?"

The amusement went out of her, replaced instantly by desire.

"Just once." It was a warning to herself more than to him.

"Just once," he agreed.

"Because…"

He dipped his head toward her, voice dropping to a whisper. "Because this is too fast."

"It's too fast," she whispered back.

"It's too hot."

"It's too hot."

His lips brushed hers. "It's too everything."

"Oh, yes."

He kissed her long and deep.

"It's not really a date," Kalissa said to Megan as they moved through the racks at Annabelle's Discount Boutique. They'd found a couple of hours to spare this morning, and it had been ages since Kalissa had bought any news clothes.

"Boy, girl, dinner, entertainment," said Megan. "What part of that is not a date?"

"I mean it's not a buy a new dress and get my hair and nails done kind of date." Kalissa held up a pair of dark blue, skinny jeans. "What do you think?"

"Cute. What's the price?"

"Thirty-nine ninety-nine, with fifty percent off."

"You can add my thirty percent off coupon."

"So, that's about fifteen bucks. I can afford fifteen bucks."

"They'll go with this," said Megan, holding up a white and silver tank top.

"I sure couldn't show up at work in that," said Kalissa.

A camera flash went off in her peripheral vision, and she turned to see two young women giggle as they looked at their phone screen then back at her.

"You like the top?" she asked them, holding it out. It was cute, but she'd give it up if they'd fallen in love with it.

They didn't answer, just gave her a thumb's up and backed away.

"What the heck?"

"It's the Darci thing," said Megan.

"What do you mean?"

"I mean, those two think they just saw the wife of a billionaire shopping at a discount store."

Kalissa glanced at the two retreating women. Suddenly self-conscious, she glanced around the store to see if anyone else was paying attention to her. They weren't, thank goodness.

"I wonder how they'd react to me using a coupon," she speculated.

"I think a lot of celebrities buy things on the cheap."

"Darci's not a celebrity."

But Kalissa now felt ridiculously conspicuous, and she glanced around the store again. Who else was out there covertly watching her? Who else might mistake her for Darci and think Darci was doing something inappropriate.

"Oh, crap." She tightened her grasp on the jeans.

"What?" Megan looked from side to side.

"Riley. The date. Me and him together at the Navy Pier."

"Those jeans will look great," said Megan. "And try on the top. I bet it works."

"What if somebody sees us? What if they think I'm Darci? What if they think she's cheating on Shane?" Kalissa had absolutely no desire to mess up anybody's life.

"It could happen," said Megan, looking thoughtful.

Kalissa put the jeans back. "Maybe I should cancel."

"You can't cancel. He seems like a great guy. And what are you going to do? Never go on a date again?"

"Maybe we could do something a little less public."

"There's always the symphony. It's dark in there."

"I have no interest in the symphony."

"Yeah." Megan nodded. "Besides, at a snooty event like that, everyone really would think you were Darci."

"This is a problem."

Megan lifted the jeans and handed them, along with the top to Kalissa. "It's not your problem."

"It's Darci's problem." Kalissa tried to work her way through the ethics of the situation. "I at least owe her something for being my sister. Don't I?"

"So, tell her."

"That I'm going on a date?"

"That you *exist*. Give her a heads up. That'll keep the reporters from blindsiding her with it."

"I could call her," said Kalissa. "Or drop her an e-mail." An e-mail sounded a lot less intimidating.

"She'll think you're a wing-nut."

"Maybe. Probably. I could send her a photo."

"She'll assume it's her, or that it's photo-shopped like you did."

Kalissa thought it through. "I could hold up today's newspaper, so she'll know that it's current."

"That would be a great way to meet her security team or maybe the Chicago Police."

"I'll phone her," said Kalissa, deciding it was the best option. "Do you suppose our voices are alike? Would she recognize it?"

"Just stop by her office," said Megan. "Colborn Aerospace has its own building down by the river. There's a huge sign."

"How do you know this?"

"I internet searched her, of course. Didn't you?"

"No. Not really. Okay, maybe a little bit. I found out she has the same birthday as me."

"Surprise, surprise."

"Just drop by her office," Kalissa pondered out loud. "Say, hi there. I'm your twin. If anyone asks you why you were on a date at the Navy Pier tomorrow, you can let them know it was me."

Megan chuckled. "Try on the jeans first. But, yeah, that's basically it."

"I could be in and out in five minutes."

"With the jeans?"

"With Darci." Kalissa couldn't quite shake the fear that any contact would be an intrusion on Darci's life. "If she doesn't want to talk. If she's too busy. I'm in, I'm out, she's warned, we're done."

"I'm guessing she might have a few questions for you."

Kalissa decided it was the best course of action. What Darci did with the information was entirely up to her. But it was colossally unfair to risk the press running with the story before Darci, and especially Shane, knew the truth.

"Shane Colborn is on line three for you," Emma Thatcher, the Ellis Aviation receptionist, announced through the inter-office phone line.

Riley moved the receiver from his ear and stared at it for a moment.

"Riley?" Emma's voice came through the tiny speaker.

"Are you sure?" he asked her.

"He claims to be Shane Colborn."

"Did he say what he wanted?"

"You want me to ask?"

"No. That's fine. I'll take it. Thanks, Emma."

"No problem."

Riley pulled his thoughts together, waiting a beat before pressing the blinking button. "Riley Ellis here."

"This is Shane Colborn."

"What can I do for you?" It was the first time Riley had spoken to his half-brother in more than a decade. They'd exchanged approximately three sentences their entire lives. And not one of them meaningful. Beyond that single moment when they were both teenagers, Shane ignored him. It was clear Shane preferred to live in denial.

"I understand you've put in a bid with Askeland Airlines."

"Where did you get that information?" Riley had no intention of either confirming or denying it.

"From Richard Price, the VP of purchasing." There was an edge of annoyance in Shane's tone. "He's hinting that your price is surprisingly low."

"You expect me to discuss my price with you? You expect me to discuss *anything* with you about a bid that may or may not exist? You have heard of collusion, right?"

The annoyance in Shane's tone ramped up. "I'm *not* asking you to collude."

"Good."

"This is a courtesy call."

Riley scoffed out a cold laugh. "So far, this seems real courteous, Colborn."

Shane's tone was a growl. "There are also laws against predatory pricing."

"Those laws are there to protect small companies. You're a billion dollar conglomerate. I'm not even a tenth of that."

"The law goes both ways."

"You'd be laughed out of court." Not that Riley was doing anything remotely illegal.

"You could be laughed into a jail cell."

"We're leaner than Colborn. That's just the way it is."

"We have a reputation for excellence."

"That and a tell-all book from your former mistress accusing you of collusion and corporate espionage. Are you spying on Ellis Aviation?"

"Don't be absurd."

"Marrying a pretty wife can't fix everything."

Shane's tone went hard. "Leave my wife out of this."

An image of Kalissa appeared in Riley's head, and guilt immediately slammed into him. Shane was right. This had nothing to do with Darci.

"You're right," he said. "I apologize."

It took Shane a moment to respond. "Everywhere I look, everywhere I turn, *you* seem to show up."

"We're in the same business," said Riley, wondering if Shane would finally acknowledge their family relationship. He lobbed him an opening. "It must be in the genes."

Again, there was a moment of silence. "Is that a crack?"

"Take it however you want."

"Inheriting something is only the first step. The place doesn't run itself."

"Inheriting is a big step," said Riley. He'd have been happy to inherit a dollar. He'd have been happy if Dalton had even once looked him in the eyes.

"I've been on my own for over six years." Shane sucked in an audible breath. "Forget it. I don't give a damn what you think."

"And I don't give a damn what you think. I bid the contracts I see fit. I've been independent since day one, and I'm planning to stay that way."

"This is strictly business?" asked Shane.

"Strictly business," said Riley.

"It feels." There was a searching tone to Shane's voice, and he paused again.

Riley hated that a mere phone call could unsettle him like this. He hated himself for hoping that Shane would acknowledge him. He'd been waiting for scraps from the Colborn table his entire life. He needed it to stop.

"Is that it?" he asked, anger crackling his tone.

"That's it," said Shane.

Riley slammed down the phone.

Three

In the lobby of the Colborn Aerospace building, Kalissa lost her nerve. She felt suddenly vulnerable in the cavernous space, phones ringing, dozens of footfalls echoing against the marble floor, men in expensive suits, women in tailored black and white. Halfway to the long, curved reception counter, she turned back.

"Mrs. Colborn," a woman approached her in a steel gray skirt and matching jacket. It was brightened by a teal blouse. "Did you get a chance to read the food services report?"

"I'm sorry," said Kalissa, her voice coming out raspy from her tight throat.

"What was that?" the woman asked. When Kalissa didn't respond, she kept on talking. "I can ride up with you on the elevator."

"Mrs. Colborn?" called another voice, a man this time.

The first woman put a hand on Kalissa's back, turning her. "Don't look up. Just keep walking and listening to me. Pretend I'm saying something absolutely riveting."

"Uh, what?" Kalissa glanced toward the voice.

"Don't look," the woman warned. She gave a nod to a security guard who moved forward to meet the man.

Another security guard held an elevator for them.

"Thank you, Bernie," said the woman as they stepped inside.

Kalissa nodded to the guard named Bernie, and he reached around to press the button for the twenty-first floor. Then he stood in front of the door until it closed. Kalissa guessed her sister and her husband didn't cram into the elevator with a dozen other people.

Her nerves ramped up even further.

"The food services report?" the woman asked.

"I'm sorry," Kalissa repeated, not knowing where else to

go with the question. She didn't want to tell some stranger she was Darci's twin before she told Darci herself. She was beginning to realize how poorly she'd thought this through.

"Not to worry," said the woman. "Give me a call when you get to it. It's all good news. The international stations are getting rave reviews, and we've had inquiries from two national food magazines about interviews. Can I tell them you'll be available?"

"Can I, uh, get back to you?" Kalissa asked weakly.

The woman peered at her. "Are you okay?"

"Just fine."

"You're not getting that flu are you?"

"I do have a bit of a headache," Kalissa replied honestly.

The elevator came to a halt, pinging at the twenty-first floor. The doors slid smoothly open.

Kalissa stepped out, not sure whether to go left or right. There was a small reception desk in the foyer, but she didn't want to ask which way it was to her office.

"Mrs. Colborn?" A woman came worriedly to her feet from behind the reception desk. She glanced down a hallway behind her, then she looked at Kalissa again. "I didn't see you leave."

Kalissa breathed a sigh of relief. At least she knew which direction to go.

"Your clothes," said the woman, bustling out from behind the desk. "Did something happen to the Farsen Kalick jacket? Do you need me to call the cleaners?"

"It's fine," said Kalissa, picking up her pace, heading for the hallway where the receptionist had looked. "I'm fine. I'll let you know."

She cleared the reception area, leaving the women behind her. She passed several closed doors. Two had nameplates on them, both belonging to vice-presidents.

At the end of the hall, she came to a set of double doors with brass handles, Shane Colborn, President. Her legs nearly gave way, and she put out a hand to brace herself against the wall. She did *not* want to run into Shane before she found Darci.

For a second, she considered turning back. But then she'd

have to face the receptionist again, and she couldn't see how she'd make it out of the building without being approached by other employees.

She straightened from the wall and took the right turn. A few moments later, she breathed a sigh of relief. She'd found it, her sister's office door: Darci Colborn, Director of Staff Services.

It was open about six inches, and she could hear Darci's voice inside. "I'll be down to the cafeteria later on."

Kalissa's stomach clenched hard, but she couldn't help a nervous smile. Darci sounded just like her.

"Okay," said Darci. "Yes, I can."

Kalissa gave a tentative knock, and the door swung further open.

Darci looked up from where she was still speaking on the phone. She leaned over for a better view, and her jaw snapped shut.

"I…" said Kalissa, not knowing where to start.

"I'll call you back," Darci said into the phone, replacing it on its cradle.

She moved around from behind the desk, taking several swift steps forward.

"I didn't mean to disturb you," said Kalissa.

"What on earth?" Darci stopped about ten feet away.

Voices sounded around the corner of the hallway, coming rapidly closer. Kalissa quickly stepped inside the office so they wouldn't see her.

"I'm so sorry," said Kalissa, regretting her decision to show up unannounced. "I thought this was the best way. But I didn't think…I didn't know…I realize this must be a bombshell for you."

"Who *are* you?" asked Darci.

"My name is Kalissa Smith. I saw your wedding pictures, and well…I guess you can figure out why I'm here."

"You look just like me."

"I know."

"I mean *exactly* like me."

"Weird, isn't it?"

Darci moved closer, peering at Kalissa.

Kalissa knew she was doing the same thing back.

Darci's eyes might be a slightly paler shade of green. But their mouths were identical, so were their chins, their noses, even their hairline. Kalissa had never come across anyone with that little swoop at their part, never mind the exact shade of auburn in their hair.

"Are we twins?" asked Darci.

"I think we must be. My birthday is October third."

Darci's eyes widened. "Holy cow."

"I didn't want to bother you," said Kalissa. "I wasn't going to say anything. I mean, I know you must be busy, being a newlywed, and with this huge company and all. But I'm going on a date tomorrow night, and there were these girls in Annabelle's Discount Boutique, and they thought I was you, and they took a photo, and I realized it could happen again, somewhere else, like the Navy Pier, while I was on a date, and people might think it was you." Kalissa clamped her mouth shut. "I'm rambling."

"We're twins," said Darci in obvious astonishment. "I don't understand. How did that happen? Were you raised by our mother? Why didn't she bring you back? And why didn't dad ever tell me that—" Darci smiled. "Now, who's rambling?"

"It's unbelievable," Kalissa whispered.

She hadn't expected to feel this way, this ache deep down in her heart. She wanted to grab Darci and pull her into a hug. She had a sister. Tears started to tingle at the backs of her eyes.

The door whooshed open behind her.

"Sweetheart," came a man's voice. "Tuck is asking if... Oh, I'm sorry."

Kalissa turned.

The man, obviously Shane, instantly froze in place.

"Darling," said Darci, a tremor in her voice. "It appears there's something more my father neglected to mention."

"What on earth?" Shane started to circle Kalissa.

"We have the same birthday," said Darci.

"Is this a con?"

Kalissa couldn't help but smile. She didn't blame Shane one bit for his suspicions. She'd have worried about him if he had accepted this at face value.

"Is she asking for money?" asked Shane.

"No," said Darci.

"I'm not," said Kalissa. "You couldn't get me to take money if you tried."

His eyes narrowed. "That's how all the best cons start off."

"Look at her," said Darci.

"We'll want DNA," said Shane.

"Take it, if you want it," said Kalissa. "But it's not necessary. I'm not going to hang around. I only wanted to warn you, well, warn Darci. Since your wedding, people have started to mistake me for her. I'm out in public. I shop at discount stores. Sometimes I swear, or get angry with a store clerk or, and this is the big one, go out on dates. I have a date tomorrow night, and I was worried I'd be mistaken for Darci. That might look bad on the two of you, and I didn't want to cause either of you any trouble."

Shane stared at her in silence.

"Thank you," said Darci. "That's very considerate of you. But seriously." She broke into a grin. Then, without warning, she rushed forward, opening her arms to pull Kalissa into a hug. "I have a twin sister."

Kalissa closed her eyes, unexplainable feelings coursing through her.

Darci drew back, cradling Kalissa's cheeks with her hands. "You are beautiful." Then she laughed. "Didn't that sound conceited."

Kalissa took in every contour of Darci's face, settling on her left cheekbone. "You have a freckle."

"You don't."

"I don't," Kalissa agreed.

Shane cleared his throat. "I'm cancelling everything for the rest of the day."

Kalissa turned to him. "Oh, no. Don't do that. I didn't plan to mess up your day."

"Of course I'm doing that. You two have a million things to talk about. We'll go to the penthouse, order some dinner. And wine. We'll need some really good wine."

"For a toast," said Darci.

Shane gave a disbelieving shake of his head. "A toast is the least of why we need the wine."

Riley could have happily done nothing but stare at Kalissa all night long. Her hair was full and shiny tonight, bouncing around her bare shoulders. Makeup brightened her beautiful face. While her tight jeans and the breezy little tank top were already giving him fantasies.

They'd snacked their way through the food kiosks and bought matching key chains with colorful, stylized letters on the fob. He'd held her hand while they navigated the crowds, waiting in a long lineup to get on the Ferris wheel. But it was worth the wait. The skies were clear, dotted with faint stars, while the skyline of Chicago was illuminated in the clear night air.

The bustle and noise of the crowds disappeared as they swept upward in the dangling car. The wind buffeted them, cooling the air temperature. Riley wrapped an arm around her, letting his fingertips brush her smooth, bare shoulder.

"I've never done this before," she told him. "Wow. Look at the city."

"You've never been up here at night?"

She shook her head. "I mean it's my first time on the Ferris wheel. I've never been to the Pier before."

"I thought you said you grew up in Chicago."

"My mom wasn't into things like this." They hit the outer apex of the curve and she grasped his arm. "This is fantastic."

Gratification swelled his chest. "No wonder you seem like a little kid."

She tilted her head to give him an unabashed grin. "Do you mind?"

"Not at all." He liked that about her. In fact, so far, he liked everything about her.

As they swung toward the top, he impulsively leaned in for a kiss. Her lips were warm and moist against his. She tasted like cotton candy, and he couldn't stop himself from taking the kiss deeper and deeper.

By the time he pulled back, they'd crested the top. Her eyes were shinning in the ride's bright lights, and her rosy cheeks had a new glow.

"I used to come here with my friends sometimes," he told her. "When I was a teenager."

It was a rare occurrence, since his childhood years hadn't held much in the way of amusement. His mother had been the runaway daughter of Irish immigrants. With only a tenth grade education, she'd worked as a housekeeper for Dalton Colborn for nearly twenty years before succumbing to a bout of pneumonia.

Determined to hold Kalissa even closer, he settled his free hand at her waist, finding a warm strip of skin at her stomach.

"Were you a wild teenager?" she asked.

"Occasionally," he admitted. "We used to street race, and we partied pretty hard. We once stole ethanol from the high school science lab. Made a killer punch that got about thirty kids blasted."

"Who's we?"

"My friend Ashton and I."

"I can picture that."

It occurred to Riley that if he wanted to impress her, he should probably change the subject from his teenage transgressions. "What about you? What were you like as a kid?"

She smoothed her hair in the wind and gave him an innocent smile. "I was good as gold."

"I don't believe you."

"It's true. I studied hard trying to get a scholarship, and I had a part time job from the time I was fourteen. I wanted to go to college, and I knew my mother could never afford it."

"So, you were the consummate good girl?"

"I was."

He moved in to playfully nuzzle her neck. "That's sexy. It makes me want to corrupt you."

She tapped him in the chest. "There's something wrong with you." But she was laughing as she said it.

"There's a whole lot wrong with me."

"Do tell."

"I don't think so."

The ground rushed up, and the car glided to a stop, giving him an easy way out of the conversation.

He exited first, then took her hand, keeping hold of it as they walked away.

"It's almost time for the fireworks," he said.

"I can't wait."

"The best view is at the far end of the pier."

"Let's go." She picked up the pace, leaning up against his arm.

He liked the feel of her against him.

The crowds had grown thinner as the evening wore on, with fewer kids darting from side to side on the walkway. They passed under strings of decorative, white lights and along yachts moored in the lake. Her hand felt good in his, but he gave in to the urge to wrap his arm around her shoulders again. She slipped hers across his back, and their thighs brushed together while they walked.

He didn't want the night to end. He wanted to take her home with him, make love to her, sure, but also hold her sleeping in his arms, talk to her over breakfast, maybe plan their Saturday together.

The vision prompted a wave of guilt. She was open and fresh and genuine, while he was a fraud, hiding the most basic of information from her.

Determined to get them on a better footing, he found a clear spot in the crowd. Then he urged her toward the rail, turning her there so they were face to face.

"What now?" Her smile was in place, but she was searching his expression with obvious confusion.

"It's Ellis," he said, ignoring his own hesitation. "My last name is Ellis."

Her smile faded, and she peered at him intently. "Are you in the witness protection program?"

"No." Where had that come from?

"I thought maybe you'd testified against a crime boss or something."

"I'm not a criminal."

"You said you were a thief."

"Ethanol. From an institution. Probably about ten bucks worth of the stuff."

Her smile came back, and her voice went sexy and low. "Riley Ellis."

Something shifted inside him.

She repeated his name.

He kissed her. It was fleeting at first, but then deeper and longer. He loved kissing her. But they were in public, so he forced himself to stop.

He rested his hands on the rails, arms around her, slowing his breathing down. "I promised you fireworks."

Her eyes were wide and clear, her lips dark red. "You meant in the sky, right? Not the ones going off inside my brain right now."

His hands twitched. "You have absolutely no sense of self-preservation."

"And you have no sense of humor."

"You are not a good girl."

"I said I was *once* a good girl." She planted a quick kiss on his mouth and then ducked under his arm.

He immediately caught her and wrapped his arm around her as they walked. "Okay, now you're taking all the fun out of the chase."

"There they go," she called out as the first red and yellow starbursts banged through the air and lit up the sky.

They quickened their pace, laughing as they went. Riley

found them a table at the beer garden, ordering beers and a savory platter.

He angled his chair toward her. He'd seen the fireworks before, but he'd never watched Kalissa watching them. The bright colors reflected off her skin and flashed in her shinning eyes. She was so much more beautiful than the display in the sky.

She caught his gaze and did a double take.

"Hey," he said softly.

"Hey."

"How do you like them so far?"

"They're stunning."

"Stunning," he agreed, his gaze fixed on her.

She glanced back at the sky, but then returned her attention to him.

"Want to know what I did yesterday?" she asked.

"Absolutely." He wanted to know everything about her.

She traced a line along her plastic beer cup. "I met Darci."

Everything went still inside Riley.

It took him a minute to respond. "Your sister?"

"Yes, my sister. Who else would I be talking about?"

He sat back in his chair.

He'd known this would happen. At one point, he'd even thought it might be good for him. He'd considered that Kalissa might give him some inside information on Shane.

But that was days ago. Now he didn't want Kalissa talking to the Colborns at all.

Riley definitely wanted to see her again.

But now that she'd met Darci, well, sisters talked, even estranged sisters were likely to talk eventually. And when they did, it was game over for him. Because the minute Shane knew Riley was in her life, he'd do everything in his power to turn her against him.

"How did it go?" he managed to ask.

"It went well, really well. They seem terrific, very down to earth, way more down to earth than I expected."

"Great," he said, covering his expression with a drink of his beer.

The fireworks popped and cracked in the distance, and the crowd oohed and aahed. Riley wanted to put his fist through the table.

Kalissa could tell something had changed. It was subtle, but Riley was quieter during the drive home, and he wasn't making any jokes. He drove directly to the Mosaic Landscaping storefront, swinging his sports car to the curb.

He hadn't suggested stopping at his place. Not that she'd wanted to stop at his place. Not that she would have said yes to stopping at his place. But there was something weird about him not even asking.

He pulled on the emergency brake, leaving the stick shift in neutral and the engine running as he exited the driver's door. He moved to her side of the car, opening the door and taking her hand while she stepped out.

"Thank you," she said, wishing this feeling of dread would go away, wishing he'd say or do something to reassure her. "I had a very nice time."

"I did too." His expression looked sincere.

What was she missing?

She took another stab. "I'm sorry I can't invite you upstairs. Megan's there and, well, it's a pretty small apartment."

The opening was a mile wide, but he didn't suggest an alternative to her place.

"I understand," he said instead, easing a little closer.

"Is something wrong?" she couldn't help asking.

"Everything's great. You're great." He tucked her hair behind one ear, sliding his palm to the back of her neck.

Anticipation warmed her skin and increased her pulse.

"Goodnight, Kalissa," he whispered. His lips came down on hers, soft and hot. But the kiss was slightly different. It didn't hold the burning passion of the ones on the Ferris wheel.

She slipped her arms around his waist, and he did the same with his free hand. Angling her body against his, she deepened the kiss. He followed suit, and she could feel his muscles hardening against her.

His hand slipped downward, splaying over her rear, pressing her into the vee of his thighs. He kissed her deeper, his tongue plunging into her mouth. She welcomed the passion, answering back, arousal growing in waves inside her.

Her imagination took flight. If not his place, maybe a hotel. His car didn't have a back seat. And she was too old for that anyway. But it had to be somewhere. He was a powerful, sexy, virile man, and the chemistry between them was all but combustible.

Then he broke the kiss, drawing back no more than an inch.

She waited for his suggestion, his solution. He had to be thinking the same thing as her.

"Goodnight, Kalissa."

As his words registered, she bit back the *yes* waiting on the tip of her tongue. She swallowed instead, letting her arms go loose around him.

"I'll see you next week?" he asked.

It was clear he meant when she came to work on his yard. "You will."

"Great." He gave her a nod. Then he stepped further back, and his gaze went meaningfully to the small door across the sidewalk.

It took her a minute to react. She opened her purse, fumbling for her keys, keeping her head down as she crossed the narrow sidewalk.

Beneath the streetlight, she pushed the key into the deadbolt lock, turning it full circle before twisting the knob and pushing the door open. As she worked up the strength to turn around, he gunned the engine, peeling away from the curb, accelerating down the empty block.

That was it. He was gone.

"Kalissa?" Megan called from the top of the stairs.

"On my way," Kalissa managed in return, swallowing her disappointment and confusion as she secured the door behind her.

Megan came down a couple of steps. "How did it go?"

"Good," said Kalissa, starting up the staircase. "Fine."

"What's wrong?"

"I don't know."

"Did he try something? Was he a jerk?"

"No, nothing like that." It was nothing even remotely like that.

Megan turned, and they filed into the one room apartment. Kalissa tossed her purse on the table and plunked down on the worn sofa.

"We had a great time," she said, walking through it in her mind.

"And?"

"He kissed me. He kissed me on the Ferris wheel, then again while we walked on the pier, then he kissed me goodnight."

Megan took the other end of the sofa. "So, why do you look so bleak?"

Kalissa was starting to question herself. "Okay, it's not like I wanted to fight him off with a stick. But he didn't make a move."

"You just said he kissed you."

"He didn't try to get me back to his place."

Megan grinned. "Let me get this straight. You're upset because he was too much of a gentleman?"

Now, Kalissa was starting to feel embarrassed. "It's always nice to be asked."

"But you would have said no."

"Yes." Kalissa paused. "Maybe. Probably. *Yes*. I would have said no. But he seemed really into me, and then pfft, this little kiss goodnight."

Megan peered at her. "Your lips are red and swollen."

Kalissa's fingertips went to her mouth. They were hot to the touch, and they did still tingle.

"He might just be a nice guy," said Megan.

"Even nice guys want sex."

"You're funny. And you're making too much of it. Did he say he'd call you?"

"He said he'd see me at his place."

"Which, he will."

"Not until Monday. Well, maybe Sunday afternoon."

Megan pulled her legs beneath her. "Ah yes, the sleepover."

"Do you think that's weird?" Kalissa asked.

"Darci wanting you to spend the night at her mansion?"

"It's less than two hours away."

"You're not going to want to drive home Saturday night. But the answer is yes. There's nothing about you going to stay at your secret, billionaire, twin sister's mansion that's not a little weird. You don't have to work at all on Sunday, you know."

"We're so busy," said Kalissa. She wasn't about to stick Megan with extra work. And she wanted to see Riley. She needed to talk to him again, to look him in the eyes and figure out exactly what had happened between them.

Four

Sunday afternoon, Riley was planted on his front steps while a dump truck noisily deposited a load of topsoil at the front of his yard. Megan appeared, caught a glimpse of him and altered her course. She trotted up the concrete staircase and sat down beside him at the top.

"How's it going?" she opened.

"It's fine." It was quite a bit below fine, but he wasn't about to share his worry with Megan.

Earlier, she'd mentioned that Kalissa had spent last night at the Colborn mansion, and Riley had been stewing ever since. He kept playing an imaginary conversation in his head, one where Kalissa told Darci she'd been on a date with Riley Ellis, and Shane reacted like a madman, warning her off, demanding she never see him again.

Maybe he shouldn't have been so quick to walk away Friday night. He sure hadn't wanted to walk away, and Kalissa had sent some pretty unmistakable signals. He should have acted on them. He should have taken her to his place to see where things would lead.

He'd worried that getting closer was a mistake. The closer he got, the more likely it was she'd mention him to Darci. But maybe that was a backward strategy. Maybe he'd blown the only chance he'd ever have to get closer to her. It might have been better if they'd spend the night together before Shane had a chance to turn her against him.

"You waiting for her?" asked Megan.

Riley fidgeted, getting the uneasy feeling Megan was reading his mind.

She glanced at her watch. "She said she'd be here around four."

A denial seemed pointless. "You've talked to her?"

"A couple of hours ago."

He swallowed, fighting his curiosity but immediately losing. "How did it go for her last night?"

"I think it went okay."

"She's in a good mood?" If Shane had told her the truth about Riley, surely she'd be angry.

Megan stood up and waved her arms to attract the attention of one of the gardeners. "The maples go in the back!" she called.

The guy nodded and strode toward a pickup truck where the workers appeared to be unloading the trees at the front of the driveway.

Megan sat back down. "You'd think they could take a minute to read the plans."

Riley couldn't care less about the yard layout. The maples could go on the roof for all he cared. He wanted to know about Kalissa.

He clenched his jaw to keep from repeating the question. He didn't want to draw attention to his curiosity.

"A good mood?" Megan asked, re-opening the topic.

"Happy?" he elaborated, feeling like he was back in high school.

"With visiting her sister?"

He gave her a sidelong glance to see if she was messing with him. What was with the third degree? "Yes, happy with visiting her sister."

"They had barbecued quail and toured some huge, dungeonesque wine cellar. Who barbecues quail? Brauts and burgers, sure. Maybe a steak. But quail? What were they trying to prove?"

"That he has more money than God."

"Shane?"

"Yes, Shane."

"I'm not even sure he was there. She sat up half the night talking with Darci."

A raw feeling of dread invaded Riley's stomach. "But she sounded okay?"

"A little tired."

This was like pulling teeth. "But not upset?"

She shifted her butt on the porch, curiosity coming into her tone. "Riley?"

"Yeah?"

She was silent until he looked her way.

"What are you doing?" she asked.

He played dumb. "What?"

"You're practically obsessing."

"I'm making conversation."

Megan tipped her chin toward the road. "There she is."

Riley's immediate reaction was relief. But it was followed quickly by trepidation.

Kalissa had parked down the block, out of the fray, and he watched her expression carefully as she approached. She was smiling. That was good, wasn't it? It had to mean he hadn't been caught.

But how long could he reasonably expect that to last? He was already operating on borrowed time. He needed to get to know her. She needed to get to know him before the bombshell was dropped.

"Do you need her here right now?" Riley asked Megan.

"What?"

"Kalissa. Can you live without her today?"

"Today's almost over."

"Is that a yes?" He came to his feet.

Kalissa was at the driveway.

"I guess, why?"

He tried to look blasé. "I wanted to take her out."

"Again? Now?"

"Yes to both."

"Where?"

"I don't know yet. Can I steal her?"

Megan gave a shrug. "If she wants. But I don't understand. She said you were a bit standoffish there at the end."

He looked Megan straight in the eyes. "That was a mistake. I've changed my mind."

A knowing smile grew on her face. "Then go for it."

Thank goodness.

He gave her a nod. "Thanks."

"No problem. Oh, good grief." She jumped up, her attention back on the gardeners. "They can't just eyeball it."

Riley's attention was solidly on Kalissa. He was walking fast, and he met her halfway up the driveway.

Her smile was tentative, definitely uncertain.

He could have kicked himself for making the wrong call Friday night. He took her hand, turning her in one smooth motion, keeping his momentum up as he headed for his car.

"What are you doing?" she asked, glancing back over shoulder.

"Let's get out of here."

She tugged on his arm. "I can't leave."

He urged her along. "Sure, you can. I checked with Megan."

"We have a bunch of work to do."

"I want to show you something."

"What?"

He had no idea. He figured he'd come up with something along the way. "It's a surprise."

He pulled out his key fob and hit the unlock button for his car door. Then he opened the passenger door, yawning it wide. "Hop in."

"This is crazy."

He smiled at her. "We'll grab something to eat."

"I can't abandon Megan."

"I told you, I already talked to Megan. Look." He nodded across the yard.

Megan, good on her, was grinning and waving goodbye.

"What's this about?" Kalissa asked, bracing her hand on the open door.

"You're not much for surprises, are you?"

"I'm not."

He scrambled for a quick answer. "I know a great little place near Lake Forest."

"Lake Forest?"

"Yes."

"We're going all the way to Lake Forest to grab something to eat."

He liked being this close to her. It didn't matter where they went. He could happily stand here on the sidewalk with her all evening long. "It'll only take an hour. And it's a nice day for a drive."

Her expression softened. "You better hope there's no traffic."

"Get in the car, Kalissa."

A light of amusement came into her eyes. "Aren't you demanding?"

He brushed the backs of his fingers along the curve of her chin. "Only when you're stubborn."

"I'm not stubborn."

"Good. Then hop in."

She looked like she was about to argue, but then she turned and settled herself in the low-slung seat.

"Thank you," he said.

"You've got me curious." She crossed her legs. They were covered in cropped black pants that were topped with a black and white checkerboard T-shirt.

He liked her shoes, black with open toes and a wedge heel. He particularly liked the wink of her toes, her slim ankles, and those toned, tanned calves.

"Riley?"

He quickly straightened, shaking off his wayward thoughts. He closed the door and crossed to the driver's side.

"I hope this is another casual spot," she said.

He started the engine, putting it into first and pulling the sports car away from the curb. Then he reached into the centre console and extracted his sun glasses.

"It's nicer than the food court," he said.

"Waiters and everything?"

"I'm hoping to redeem myself."

"I had a lot of fun at the pier."

"I know. I'm talking about the way I behaved after the pier." He figured there was no point in letting it simmer.

"Did something go wrong?" she asked, canting herself in the seat so she was looking directly at him.

He pulled the car to a stop at the light leading onto Hamilton, flipping on his left signal. "I didn't want to push you."

It was true. It might not be the whole truth, but it was definitely true.

"You'd rather I pushed you."

He turned his head to take in her forthright expression. "I promise you, that'll never happen again."

"I can't see your eyes."

He pulled off his glasses to make his intentions crystal clear. "That'll *never* happen again."

"Good to know." Her gaze flicked out the windshield. "Light's green."

A horn sounded behind him.

It was pretty clear to Kalissa that the drive was going to take more than an hour. Riley had chosen the scenic route, taking secondary roads that meandered along the lakeshore.

"How did it go with Darci last night?" he asked her as they made their way past a beach. The strip of park was quiet except for the wind blowing through the oak trees and the whitecaps crashing on shore.

"How did you know about last night?"

"Megan mentioned it. She said you went to the mansion."

Kalissa smiled at the memory. "That's some house they've got out there."

"Big?" asked Riley.

"Humongous."

"I guess that's what you can buy when you're a billionaire."

"Shane doesn't seem like a billionaire."

Sure, he had nice clothes and expensive real estate, and she was pretty sure Darci had said something last night about a private jet. But if you'd met him at a shopping mall or on the street, you'd never know.

Riley looked skeptical "How does he not seem like a billionaire?"

"He's pretty down to earth."

"He's trying to impress you."

"I don't see why he'd care."

"Maybe because you're Darci's twin sister?"

"He seems genuine."

"I doubt that."

The flip remark annoyed her. "How would you know? You've never even met him."

"I met him once," said Riley, an edge to his voice. "In passing. A long time ago." He paused. "I'm sure he's changed."

"Why are you doing that?"

"Doing what?"

"Giving in with your teeth clenched. If you want to fight with me, fight with me."

"I don't want to fight with you."

"You've obviously got something against Shane. Or are you jealous of his money?"

"He's just one more rich guy in Chicago."

"Well, I'm a little jealous of his money." Not that Kalissa had any interest in a mansion. But she'd love to pay down Mosaic's line of credit. And she could sure get used to that wine cellar.

"He'll probably give you some of it," said Riley.

"I should sock you for that one."

"Not while I'm driving. But later, if you like."

"I wouldn't take his money if he forced it on me. Just because there's some random, genetic connection between me and Darci—"

"She's your identical twin."

"I know that."

"That's hardly random."

"My point is, being related to her doesn't give me any call on their wealth. That's one of the reasons I tried to stay away from her. I knew everybody would think I was after her money. I'm incredibly grateful that Darci and Shane at least don't think I'm a gold digger."

"I don't think you're a gold digger."

"Then why are we arguing about it?"

"You're the one who brought it up."

"I did not."

"You said you were jealous of his money."

She realized Riley was right. "I didn't mean it that way."

"Okay."

"I meant it in a theoretical, fantasy-like way. Who wouldn't want a little extra money to toss around?"

"I'd take a little extra money." Riley slowed the car and pulled off the road into a wide parking lot.

"What are you doing?"

"I'm thirsty."

He maneuvered the car into an empty parking stall close to a grassy, tree lined area of the park. The branches swayed in the wind, and there was a strip of sandy beach on the far side of the lawn, with big foaming waves rushing up onto it.

"We could take a walk on the beach," he suggested.

She couldn't help but smile at that. "Have you been brushing up on dating?"

"Huh?"

"Long walks on the beach. I'm pretty sure that's the number one documented female dating fantasy. We expect you to pour out your heart and soul to us, while holding our hands, scampering in the waves, and looking like a guy in a hair products' commercial."

His brows went up. "Scamper?"

"Yes."

"I did not know any of that."

She gave him a smirk. "Are you afraid to scamper?"

He reached down to untie the laces of his hikers, heaving a long-suffering sigh. "I'll do what I have to do."

She realized he was serious about walking. "I've never seen it done during a gale force wind."

He glanced out the windshield. "It doesn't look so bad."

She retrieved her purse from beside her feet, opening it to search for a stray ponytail elastic. "Probably no more than sixty knots. But I am thirsty."

"That's the spirit. I'd say forty-five knots, tops."

While he peeled off his boots, Kalissa fastened her hair and kicked off her sandals.

They got out of the car into the breeze. Luckily, it was warm. In fact, it was kind of refreshing.

She tipped her chin and let the sunshine caress her face.

Riley slipped his hand into hers, and they started across the thick grass to the concession stand.

Halfway there, a black lab bounded toward them. It dropped a stick at their feet and wagged its tail, brown eyes looking eagerly up.

Riley let go of Kalissa's hand and picked up the stick. He gave it a mighty throw, sending it spiraling in a high arc to land on an empty stretch of sand.

"That's some arm," she told him.

"I was a pitcher for a while in high school."

"Were you good?"

"Not bad. There were other guys who were better."

She found her sympathies engaging. "Did you get cut from the team?"

"No." He gave her a playful shove with his hip. "I did not get cut from the team. I had too much studying to do senior year, so I didn't try out."

"What were you studying? Where did you go to college?"

"I stayed in Illinois. IIT Armour College."

"Nice. I went to community college, got a diploma not a degree. I was pretty much on my own for money. Well, I was completely on my own for money."

The dog loped toward them again, returning the stick.

Riley threw it once more.

"You like dogs?" Kalissa asked.

"I do."

"Did you have them growing up?"

He shook his head. "Pets were not one of my mother's priorities."

"What about your dad? Brothers and sisters?"

His gaze was on the dog as it picked up the stick. "Just me and my mom. It wasn't Norman Rockwell."

"Same with me," she said. "Which isn't unusual for adopted kids."

"Was it lonely for you?" he asked, taking her hand again.

"It was. She, uh…" Kalissa hesitated. She didn't like to broadcast her past. But it sounded like Riley had been there himself.

"My adopted dad died when I was five. My mother never really recovered. She drank after that. Quite a lot. So I pretty much raised myself."

He gave her hand a small squeeze. "My mother worked. She didn't have the skills to make much money, so she was gone for long hours. I hear you on raising yourself."

"How could you afford IIT?"

"I was lucky enough to get a scholarship."

"So, quitting baseball worked for you."

"It did."

"I wasn't smart enough to get more than a community college scholarship." She wasn't indulging in self-pity. It was just a fact.

"Don't sell yourself short. Your intellect gives me a run for my money."

She appreciated the sentiment. "I'm beginning to doubt that."

"It wasn't brilliance that got me there. I studied my butt off in senior year. I had my head in textbooks every waking minute."

"I worked weekends and most evenings in high school."

If she hadn't, they never would have made the rent on their modest basement suite. By that time, her mother was drunk every day, and welfare checks alone would never have covered their living expenses.

The dog was back again, dropping the stick.

"He knows you're a soft touch," said Kalissa.

Riley hurled the stick. "He'll wear out eventually."

"Thank goodness you can throw so far."

"If you'd had time to study," said Riley, "You could have won any scholarship you wanted."

She didn't buy it for a second.

"I can tell," he said.

"You cannot."

"How were your grades?"

"Fine. I guess they were good."

"How good?"

"A's and B's," she admitted.

She'd been lucky enough to have a knack for most subjects. It made up for her lack of time to study around her part time job. But high school coursework was nothing compared to college.

"I rest my case," he said. "Soda good for you?"

They had arrived at the little concession stand set amongst a dozen wooden picnic tables.

"You have no case. Soda sounds great."

Riley stepped up and placed their order.

"You think you'll ever get a dog?" Kalissa asked while they waited.

"I will someday. Maybe when I'm settled, when the business is running well, and I have a family."

"You want a family?"

"Yes, I do. I want a wife, a couple of kids, and a white picket fence. I want to create what I never had growing up."

"Norman Rockwell?"

"A modern version."

The young man behind the counter handed them two cardboard cups filled with ice and cola.

"If you need any landscaping," Kalissa joked as they strolled away.

"You'll be my first call."

"Unless you're planning to stay in the house you've got. It's going to look great. Well, from the outside." She hadn't seen much of the inside, only the basement.

His tone turned intimate. "You'll have to come and see the rest of it."

She looked up, meeting his dark eyes, and her heart gave a couple of quick beats. "You think?"

"I know."

The dog dropped the stick beside Riley's feet, and Kalissa's phone rang in her pocket.

He quickly got rid of the stick again.

"It's Megan," said Kalissa.

He surprised her by whisking the phone out of her hand.

"Hey," she protested.

He put it to his ear. "Megan? Yeah. Can this wait?"

"Give that back," said Kalissa.

"Uh-huh," he said into the phone.

Kalissa leaned in to call out. "Megan? Megan, I'm here."

"Don't be melodramatic," Riley said to Kalissa. "She is," he said into the phone. Then he gave a mischievous grin. "No, we're not."

"What's she asking?" Kalissa stage whispered.

"What do you think?" he asked her.

Kalissa called into the phone again. "We're in public, on the beach."

"How would you feel about Kalissa turning this thing off for a while?" Riley asked Megan.

"I'm not turning my phone off," said Kalissa.

"Okay," said Riley.

"Good," said Kalissa.

"I was talking to Megan."

"I'm not turning it off."

"Great," said Riley. "Thanks." He ended the call.

"Hey!"

"She's fine with you turning it off."

"I'm not turning it off."

Megan's calls were probably the only ones that might be important, but she could get other calls. Her sister, for example.

"I will if you will," said Riley.

"No."

"Let's pretend we're out of tower range."

"Like if we were hiking the Adirondacks?"

He handed her phone back then drew his own out of his pocket. He moved his way through the screens.

"There," he said. "Mine's off." He waited.

"I didn't agree to this."

"This is a lot like hiking the Adirondacks. Except there'll be plumbing, fine china, and a Maitre-de."

A Maitre-de? "Where, exactly are you taking me?"

"Turn off your phone. You can do it, Kalissa."

Something was making her hesitate. But there was no reason to refuse. If Megan knew she was out of touch, nobody would worry if they couldn't reach her. "If I turn it off, you'll tell me where we're going?"

"Absolutely."

She gauged his expression. "Tell me first."

"You don't trust me?"

"I don't."

He gave a long suffering sigh. "It's a restaurant called the Trestle Tree. It's in a historic building on the lakeshore. It used to belong to a railway baron."

"I've never heard of it."

"You think I'm making it up?"

"I think I don't know much more than I did two minutes ago."

"Maybe, but I kept my side of the bargain."

He had her there.

She gave in and shut down her phone.

Five

"I'm not going in there," said Kalissa, one hand resting on the dashboard.

Riley didn't understand. "I ate there once a couple of years ago. It's really nice inside."

As far as he was concerned, it was nice outside too, a four-story, red brick, historic building, lined with arched windows and decorated with a narrow wrought iron balcony along the second floor. It was illuminated by pot lights and spotlessly maintained, with a gleaming white concrete staircase and trimmed plants bracketing a green and glass double door.

"I'm talking about the people," she said.

"What's wrong with the people?"

A man in a neat business suit was escorting two women up the short staircase. He looked to be in his fifties. One woman was about the same age. The other looked to be in her twenties. A daughter, Riley guessed. He didn't see a single thing wrong with them.

"Are you blind?"

He assumed it was a rhetorical question, but he answered anyway. "No."

"The dresses, Riley. Look at their dresses."

"What about them?"

One woman was in royal blue, the other in black.

"Now, look at me." She gestured to herself.

"You look fantastic."

She did. The simple black slacks clung to the curve of her hips, and the white top showed off her tan. Her hair was only slightly windswept. Her green eyes sparkled beneath the streetlight, and her face seemed to get more beautiful by the minute.

"I'm wearing jeans."

"Those aren't jeans."

"They're black, but they are jeans. And look at you?"

He glanced down at his khaki pants. Okay, they weren't exactly formal, but they were clean.

"You look like you walked off a shop floor."

"I did."

"Exactly. Let's go somewhere else, maybe a café or a drive-through."

"You want me to take you to a drive-through?"

Like he was going to trump Shane by taking her to a drive-through. No way. Tonight was about impressing her, showing her his better qualities before Shane could enumerate his failings.

"We could grab a burger and find a nice park for a picnic."

"We're not going to a drive-through. Look at those people." He pointed to a party of four on the sidewalk. "They're more casually dressed."

"Nice try."

Okay, so maybe it was a stretch. The men were both wearing blazers, but the women's dresses were much shorter and less formal.

He glanced around for a solution.

Then he saw it.

"If I change?" he asked.

She frowned. "Into what?"

He pointed two doors down the street to a clothing store.

She chuckled, obviously assuming it was a joke. "You're going to buy new clothes?"

"Why not?"

"Because that's a crazy idea."

He opened the door. "Let's at least go look."

"You're a crazy person," she called from behind him.

But she climbed out of the car.

He waited for her and held out his hand.

"I don't know why I humor you," she muttered.

"Lighten up."

"I am light. At least I'm usually light." She paused. "Fine.

Okay. I'll stop complaining. What's the worst that can happen?"

He raised her hand and kissed it while they walked. "That's the spirit."

"You're mocking me."

"You're pretty easy to mock."

When they made it to the store, he pushed the door open.

Inside, it was long and narrow, done in grey tones with muted lighting. It featured men's dress shirts, slacks and sport coats down one side, with ladies skirts, blazers and classic blouses down the other.

"The women's wear looks a bit conservative," he whispered in her ear. "But see what they've got."

"I'm not going to—"

He shot her a mock scowl. "If I'm going to look dressier, you have to make an effort too."

She held up her hands in surrender. "Okay, okay. I'm not complaining."

"Glad to hear it."

A woman approached them. "Can I help you?"

"Do you have any dresses?" Riley asked her.

"We do," she answered brightly. "It's a small collection. They're closer to the back. This way."

It didn't take Riley long to find slacks, a shirt and a jacket that would fit him. He left the new things on and dropped the tags and his old clothes at the checkout counter. Then he headed to the back of the store to find Kalissa.

She was emerging from a changing cubical in a simple, short black dress. It looked nice, mostly because it was Kalissa inside. But it seemed a bit boring.

"My shoes will work with this," she said to the clerk.

"Do you have anything with some color?" asked Riley, glancing at the racks beside him.

"You don't like it?" asked Kalissa. "It's very versatile."

He lifted a frothy, bright blue dress with a single, jeweled shoulder strap. "What about this?"

She looked aghast. "I'm not buying that."

"You're not buying anything. I am. Try it on."

The clerk grinned at the exchange.

Kalissa opened her mouth, but he beat her to the punch.

"What else do you have?" he asked the clerk. "She needs something pretty. We're going to a very important dinner."

"You're nuts," said Kalissa.

"You promised you wouldn't complain," he countered.

"You want me to stand here and shut up while you spend a fortune on a dress I'm only going to wear once?"

"Now you're catching on."

The clerk's grin grew wider, and she put a hand on Kalissa's arm, her voice reflecting a wise tone. "Honey, there are times when you simply keep quiet and let a man have his way. This is one of them."

Kalissa hit Riley with a stern stare. "Is that truly what you want me to do?"

"Absolutely." He couldn't stop a smile. He might not be Shane, but he wasn't impoverished either. He could indulge her in whatever fancy dress she wanted. "Feel free to accessorize."

She rolled her eyes, but held out her hand for the blue dress.

"I'll see what else we have," the clerk cheerfully added.

Riley waited while Kalissa changed.

When she emerged, he gave a low whistle. The fabric gathered softly across her breasts, with a weave of jewels swooping under the bodice, up to the single shoulder strap, leaving plenty of bare skin. Man, he loved her shoulders.

Beneath the bodice, soft, translucent fabric fell to a scalloped hem at mid-thigh, revealing her smooth, toned legs.

"That's the one," he said.

The clerk arrived and glanced down at an armful of dresses.

"You've decided?" she asked.

"What do you think?" he asked Kalissa.

"It kind of works." There was a glow to her expression.

"We'll take it," he said.

"I have some silver shoes," said the clerk. "The black is rather jarring."

"I don't—" said Kalissa.

"Sure," said Riley.

"I'll be right back," said the clerk.

Kalissa pursed her lips.

"No complaints," Riley warned.

"I'm not saying a word."

She turned to look in a three way mirror, and Riley's knees almost gave way. Her back was very nearly bare, a large diamond shape was cut out between the bodice and the skirt. It was the sexiest thing he'd ever seen.

The clerk returned with the shoes, and Kalissa sat down to try them on. Even before she stood up, he knew they were perfect, slim, high heels, a silver sheen, and little straps around her ankles. Forget dinner, he wanted to carry her off to the nearest bedroom.

She rose, and he joined her in front of the big mirror, deciding she looked perfect next to him.

"Do you think they'll let us in the restaurant now?" he asked.

"Where are you going?" asked the clerk.

"The Trestle Tree."

"Oh, you've hit it just right."

"He wanted me to wear jeans." Kalissa told the woman.

"Buying new clothes was my idea," Riley pointed out.

Kalissa just smiled at her reflection, swaying ever so slightly so that the hem brushed her legs.

The clerk frowned. "You can't wear jeans to the Trestle Tree."

"Noted," said Riley.

"It seems we make a good team," Kalissa teased.

"You're strategic direction, and I'm implementation."

"That sounds about right."

It was right. They were right together. And he wanted to keep the togetherness going for a long, long time.

The wind had died down, and after they'd finished eating, Kalissa had moved with Riley to the patio overlooking the lake. They were standing at the rail under a starry sky, sipping coffees laced with brandy, sugar and whipped cream.

It felt decadent. She felt decadent. Everything about the evening felt decadent, from the wild mushroom and goat cheese appetizer to the cedar planked salmon. And the dress, she loved her new dress. She especially loved the way Riley's fingertips now brushed her bare back.

"This was nice," she told him. "Thanks for talking me into it."

"Thanks for coming along." His lips brushed her temple.

It was the simplest of kisses, but it sent a reaction skittering over her skin. She was intensely attracted to him. She liked his looks, his voice, and his scent. She particularly liked his mind, his intelligence and agile wit.

He held his own against her sarcasm and challenges. Most men either backed off or became genuinely angry. As a teenager, she'd tried to temper that facet of her personality, having been told by friends and often by her mother that she'd frighten boys off. But she didn't want to change. She wanted to be strong.

But then, sometimes she wanted to be soft. She set her coffee down on the stand-up table beside them and leaned her head against his chest.

He followed suit, getting rid of his own cup.

"No pressure," he said. "Believe me, the last thing I want to do is make you uncomfortable."

She smiled to herself. "Okay."

"But, up there."

She looked, and found him gazing at the three stories above them. Lights shone from some of the windows.

"They have guest rooms," he continued. "I saw a sign with a picture on the way in, and they look very nice."

"You're suggesting something?" Already her pulse had jumped. Her skin warmed and a thrill of arousal swirled inside her.

He looked down, meeting her eyes in the darkness. "I'm not going to leave it to you this time."

"To push?"

"I'm pushing," he said, his head dipping toward her. "You can say no, but I'm definitely the one pushing tonight."

He kissed her, and her desire ramped up. She didn't want to say no. She wasn't going to say no. Riley was amazing, and she was dying to spend the night in his arms.

She drew back. "Let's see if they have a room."

A glow came into his dark eyes. His hand closed over hers, and he led her from the rail, back through the restaurant and into the lobby of the inn.

"Checking in?" asked the man behind the reception counter.

"We don't have a reservation," said Riley.

The man hit a few keys on the terminal in front of him. "Let's see what we have available."

"With a view if that's possible," said Riley.

"We have a junior suite with a king sized bed, a connected seating area, and floor to ceiling windows overlooking the lake."

"We'll take it," said Riley, giving her hand a squeeze.

Her heart kicked up, her chest tightening with exhilaration and just a touch of anxiety.

After checking in, they took a creaking, ancient elevator to the fourth floor. Then they followed a scuffed and uneven hardwood floor hallway to the end before finding their room.

"The rooms looked nice on the lobby poster," said Riley, a touch of worry in his tone as he wiggled the metal key into the deadbolt lock and turned.

The heavy door squealed as it swung open.

He fumbled for the light switch, found it, and the big room came into view.

It didn't disappoint.

"It's gorgeous," Kalissa breathed, stepping inside to look around the airy space.

The carpet was plush beneath her feet. A pristine, blue and gold striped Victorian sofa was bracketed by two matching armchairs, the arrangement set in front of a marble fireplace with a hearth that stretched to the high ceiling. A huge brass bed was positioned in an alcove, the head decorated by rich fabric, draped on the wall. In the center of the room, the ceiling was domed, carved and painted white, matching the scrolls of the crown molding above abstract blue and copper wallpaper.

Throw pillows were everywhere, including on a bay window bench seat that overlooked the dark lake. Heavy curtains hung from brass rings above six massive windows. The colorful pillows all but buried a thick quilt on the bed.

She turned a lever on one of the windows, and the catch came free.

"Look at this," she said, pushing the window wide to let in the fresh air.

"Look at this," said Riley in a low, reverent tone.

She turned.

He was gazing intently at her. The expression in his eyes was passionate and possessive.

"You don't want to check out the room?" she asked.

"Not really." He moved forward.

"You want to check out the bed?"

"I do."

She snuck past him to the mound of pillows that buried the white quilt. "You think we can *find* the bed?"

In answer, he scooped her into his arms.

"Hey."

Before she knew what was happening, he'd placed her in the middle of the pillow pile.

"I found it," he said, lowering himself to the edge of the bed.

"I don't think I can move in all this."

"You don't have to move."

His hand skimmed down her calf, coming to the buckle on her new shoe. "I love these."

"I think I'm getting blisters."

"Poor you." He released the strap, easing off the shoe.

"Oh, that feels *good.*"

"So, I'm off to a promising start?" He switched to the other shoe.

"You're off to a fantastic start."

"Glad to hear it."

He lifted her bare foot, bending her knee, then leaned forward to place a kiss on her ankle. "Better?"

"Better."

He worked his way up her calf, making small circles with his thumb. Her skin warmed under his touch, the warmth turning to arousal as he massaged the back of her knee. When his hand moved up her thigh, the arousal turned to need.

"Riley," she breathed.

He stretched out beside her, his palm moving to her rear, cupping her silk panties. He smoothed her hair back from her face, coming closer.

"You're amazing," he whispered.

"I'm not doing anything."

"Yes, you are."

She touched his shoulder, marveling at its strength, moving her hand down his arm, memorizing the definition of his muscles. She cupped the hand that was at her cheek, loving the textured skin, the wide palm, the strong, blunt fingers.

She turned her head and kissed his palm, tasting it with the tip of her tongue.

He groaned.

Then he kissed her exposed neck, slowly making his way to her shoulder with a pattern of hot kisses.

She let her head fall back, clinging tight to his hand, letting the arousing sensations wash over her.

He drew back, gazing into her eyes. Then he zeroed in on her mouth, and passion overtook her. Her arms went around his neck, holding him tight. His kisses were long and deep. His hand stopped on her rear, then it fisted around her panties, dragging them down.

She kicked them off.

He slipped her single shoulder strap down, kissing behind it and nudging the dress aside to expose her breasts. Her nipples went taut beneath his kiss. They tingled, sending bands of want straight to her abdomen.

She blindly reached for the buttons on his shirt, awkwardly popping them from their holes, pushing his shirt off, and pressing her skin to his.

He hugged her tight, rolling so that she was sprawled over his chest, her hair dangling in a curtain around his face. He kissed her mouth again, pulling up on her dress, breaking the kiss just long enough to remove it and toss it aside.

She was naked then, and he was hot and so incredibly sexy. She pushed herself up, sitting astride him.

"You are incredible," he whispered reverently, cupping her breasts.

She tipped back her head, and her toes curled in.

"You have a condom," she managed.

"I do."

Relieved, she popped the button on his slacks. She drew down the zipper. He bracketed her hips, holding her firmly against him as his hips rotated beneath her.

She didn't think she'd ever been this aroused.

Then his hands moved to her thighs, stroking their way up. She cried out when they met, buckling with the sensation.

She dragged down his pants, and he kicked them off, donning the condom.

"Like this?" she asked, positioning herself on top again.

"Like anything," he groaned, grasping her hips and pulling her home.

Energy raced through her body. She rocked against him, over and over again.

"This is incredible," he ground out. "*You* are incredible. I'm not. I can't."

She leaned in to kiss him, capturing his tongue and returning with hers. His hands roamed her body, finding secret places that made her twitch and buck with reaction.

Finally, he flipped them over, bracing the small of her back, pulling her into him as he thrust forward harder and harder, increasing their speed. Warmth glowed in the base of her brain, getting hotter and brighter.

The world disappeared. Nothing existed but Riley, his

breath in her ear, the scent of his skin, the feel of his body as he pulled hers to unimaginable heights.

She groaned as she hovered for a long, long moment.

"Kalissa," he cried, his body convulsing within her.

She crashed over the edge, spiraling downward in pure ecstasy.

"Riley," she gasped, hoping he'd catch her, knowing he'd catch her.

His arms were solid steel around her, and slowly the freefall ended, the soft pillows cushioning her.

Her heartbeat was wild. His heart thudded in return.

They both breathed deeply.

His body was a hot weight on top of her. It felt good. She felt safe. She never wanted him to leave.

"Wow," he said, smoothing back her hair. "Just...wow."

"I'm not going to argue with that."

"Well, that's a switch." There was a clear smile in his voice.

"You are *so* brave to tease me."

He lifted his head. "Am I too heavy?"

"No." She looked into his eyes. "I like it."

"Oh, man. Kalissa." He kissed her.

Then he kissed her again, and again, each one longer and deeper.

His hand covered her breast again, and her nipple hardened to a peak.

"Can we?" he asked in a strained voice.

"Yes," she answered. "Oh, yes."

In the early morning sunrays, Riley watched through half closed eyes as Kalissa eased up on her elbow beside him. Her hair was tousled, and the pure white pillow and comforter billowed around her. She gazed at him in silence.

"What are you thinking?" he asked.

"You're awake." Her voice was husky with sleep.

"I am."

"Did I wake you?"

"No. What are you thinking?"

She paused. "I was thinking it never happens this way."

He loved the sound of her voice. The words didn't even have to make sense. "What never happens which way?"

She cracked an obviously self-conscious smile. "You meet a guy. He's smart, funny, good looking, and then…" A delightful touch of pink flushed her cheeks.

"Sometimes it happens that way." And he was beyond thrilled that it had.

"There's always a catch."

He agreed with that. "Catch is." He settled a hand on her bare hip. "I'm falling for you."

Her smile widened. "That's not a catch."

It was for him, and that was the hard truth. He was quickly coming to care for her, but he was destined to upset and disappoint her. There was no way around it.

But not now, he told himself, not today. There was still some more time before the real world crowded in.

She glanced behind him and her expression sobered. "We're late."

He realized she'd glimpsed the bedside clock. "I disagree. We're right on time."

"I'm late for work." She gave a longing glance around the picturesque room. "I'm late for my real life."

He slipped an arm beneath her, determined to hold her in place. "Real life's over-rated."

"Maybe so, but mine's out there waiting for me."

"Let it wait." Deep down, he knew he'd never have another chance like this.

She sat up, giving him a lovely profile view of her breasts and the indentation of her stomach.

"I can't abandon Megan."

He rose beside her, searching for the words that would change her mind. Then he spotted her cell phone on the bedside table. He reached for it and swiftly opened her contacts. There was Megan.

He connected a call and put it to his ear.

Kalissa obviously heard something, and she turned to look at him. Her brows knitted in confusion.

"Hey, you," came Megan's sing-song voice. "How'd it go?"

"It's Riley," he said.

Megan's tone immediately changed. "What's wrong?"

"Nothing's wrong. Kalissa's right here."

"Who are you talking to?" asked Kalissa, her confusion obviously growing.

"Where's here?" asked Megan.

"Lake Forest."

"What are you doing way out there?"

"Hey," Kalissa called. "That's *my* phone."

"Tell her hi," said Megan.

"Megan says hi," Riley told Kalissa.

"Give it back." Kalissa lunged forward.

He leaned away from the bed, reaching for her shoulder to hold her at arm's length.

"I was hoping to keep her for a while," he said to Megan.

"I'm taking a shower, then we're coming home." Kalissa called out so that Megan would hear. She was obviously trying to glower at him, but the amusement in her eyes was giving her away.

"She's taking a shower?" asked Megan.

"No." Riley hesitated, wondering how much he ought to reveal. "I, uh, just came in and woke her up."

"Oh, good grief," said Kalissa. "She's not going to buy that. Give me the phone."

"Do you need her right away?" asked Riley.

"Tell her to have fun," said Megan.

"Give me that phone," said Kalissa, punctuating her words by bopping him in the shoulder with the heel of her hand. Her lips twitched as she clearly fought a smile.

"Megan says to have fun."

"I am *not* going to have fun."

He grinned in triumph. "You're already having fun."

"You should probably let her talk to me," said Megan.

"Okay," Riley agreed. "But you're my wing-man in this."

Megan laughed.

Riley handed the phone to Kalissa.

"Hey," Kalissa said into it, giving Riley a stern glare.

He pulled her close, folding her against his chest.

To his delight, she didn't fight him.

"It was nice," she said to Megan.

"Nice?" Riley growled in an undertone.

She elbowed him in the ribs.

"That's nuts," she said to Megan. "We'll head back right away."

"Tell her I'll have you home by tonight," said Riley.

"She can hear you," said Kalissa.

"Is she agreeing?" asked Riley.

"She's not the person you have to convince," said Kalissa.

Then she took the phone from her ear.

Megan's voice was tinny but audible. "Do you two even need me in this conversation?"

"Yes," said Kalissa.

"No," said Riley.

Megan gave a spurt of laughter. "Take the day. You sure deserve it."

"So do you," said Kalissa.

"I'll take one later."

There was hesitation in Kalissa's expression. She looked up at Riley.

He gave her an encouraging smile and ran his fingertips from the tip of her smooth shoulder, over her collarbone and up her neck.

Her head tipped ever so slightly, and her eyes closed.

"Fine," she breathed in capitulation.

"Thank you, Megan," Riley called.

"You can't have her forever," warned Megan.

"We'll see you tonight," he answered, lifting the phone from Kalissa's unresisting hand and ending the call.

As he gazed at her creamy skin, her gorgeous hair and those full luscious lips, he thought forever sounded about right.

Six

In an open air art market, in a historical section of Lake Forest, they found some dramatic metal sculptures. Kalissa knew they'd be perfect for Riley's patio. After a brief protest, he agreed to buy them. He was now lugging the two unwieldy pieces toward his car.

His phone rang, and he glanced down at his pants pocket.

"You want me to?" Kalissa asked, tentatively reaching.

"Can you just tell me who it is?" He shifted the sculptures to give her access.

She reached into the pocket, taking a moment to get her hands on the phone.

His eyes twinkled. "Keep looking."

"You have a one track mind."

"I do around you."

She managed to extract the phone, lifting it to check the display.

"Wade Cormack?" she told him.

Riley blew out a sigh. "I'd better take that." He glanced around, spotting a bench under a tree. "It's a business associate. Can you tell him to hang on?"

"Sure." Kalissa pressed the answer button. "This is Riley Ellis's phone," she answered as she followed him toward the bench.

"And who is this?" The man's voice was smooth and professional.

"This is Kalissa Smith. He'll just be a moment."

"Are you his new secretary?" asked Wade Cormack.

Kalissa hesitated, wondering how exactly she would describe herself. "Something like that. I'm on contract."

Riley set down the sculptures and gave her a look of confusion.

"What kind of a contract?" asked Wade.

"Mr. Ellis is ready for you now," she said in a very proper voice, grinning as she handed over the phone.

Riley listened for a moment. "She's none of your business, that's who she is."

Kalissa chuckled as she plopped down on the bench next to the sculptures. His gardener? His date? His one night stand? All were true one way or another.

"No," said Riley, his voice rising. "Of course not. Give me a break."

His expression sobered. He glanced at Kalissa, then he turned and took a couple of steps away.

She tried not to listen to what was obviously a confidential call, but his voice carried.

"How did you find that out?" asked Riley, bracing his feet apart.

Kalissa focused her attention on the clusters of people walking past, couples, families, some with strollers, many of them carrying paintings and other packages.

"Crap," Riley spat in a tone of disgust.

Kalissa found herself sitting up straight, taking in his tense posture. Whatever had happened, it obviously wasn't good, and it seemed like their stolen day away was about to end.

She was disappointed by that. Having worked through her guilt at leaving Megan on her own, she'd started to hope Riley would suggest stopping for dinner on the way back to Chicago.

"As soon as I can," said Riley. "Maybe somewhere overseas?"

His head nodded. "I know. He'll have thought that through too. Damn-it."

Kalissa's emotions wavered between pity and curiosity.

"I'll let you know," said Riley.

He turned back, shoving his phone into his pocket.

She came to her feet. "Do we need to go back?"

"What?" He was obviously distracted.

"Do we need to go back? Are you in a hurry?"

"It's all right," he said, gathering up the sculptures.

"It's okay if you do," she told him. "It wouldn't hurt for me to check up on—"

"There's a guy," said Riley as they started their way back down the pedestrian street. "He's a competitor. He paid a 'rush' premium to buy up all the stock on a particular part that he doesn't really need from three different suppliers. So they've back-ordered on me."

"Why would he do that?"

"To shut down my assembly line and destroy my company."

"That's appalling."

Riley stared straight ahead, his pace increasing as he talked. "He's a very competitive man."

"He sounds like a bona-fide jerk."

Riley's jaw clenched tight, and they walked in silence for the next block.

"What are you going to do?" she asked.

"Try to find another source for the part."

"Can you do anything to him? Take him to court maybe. Is it illegal?"

"It's not illegal. It's ruthless, and it's definitely smart."

She was surprised that Riley would have anything positive to say about the man.

"Smart?" she asked.

"Brilliant, actually. I didn't see it coming."

"Who is he?" she asked.

Riley's expression relaxed. "Nobody important. Definitely nobody you need to worry about."

"If he can destroy your company…" How could that fail to make him important?

"If a competitor can destroy my company that easily, I don't deserve to succeed."

"Seriously?"

"Seriously. Tell me, what would you do if another landscaping company bought up all of the, say, Boxwood?"

She came up with a quick solution. "I'd substitute Privet."

"If you couldn't substitute? What if every customer you had demanded a Boxwood hedge as part of the garden design?"

"I'd order from out of state."

"And if there was none available out of state?"

She thought about it for another moment. "Well, it would take a while, but I could start a nursery and grow my own."

It took her a second to realize that Riley had stopped walking. She turned back. "What?"

"You'd grow your own," he said, a calculating look in his eyes.

"It would take a while. And I'm assuming I could get my hands on some seed."

"I can get seed," he said.

She wondered if she'd lost sight of the overall metaphor. "Are you saying you want a Boxwood hedge?"

His attention moved back to her. "What?"

"We're not seriously talking about a hedge?"

His brow furrowed. "No."

"I thought maybe I'd missed a left turn in the conversation. We're still talking about you. The seeds aren't literally seeds."

"They're not seeds." He began walking again.

She trotted a couple of steps. "So, what are they?"

"A titanium alloy, C-110M."

She rolled that one over in her mind. "What exactly is it you do, Riley?"

"It's not as complicated as it sounds. It's just a type of metal. If we have approved specs, we can contract someone to make the part. It'll be expensive, and it'll take some time, but it's not impossible."

They'd arrived at the car, and he popped the small truck. "Well, this is going to be a tight fit."

She took in the space and the shape of the sculptures.

"Turn that one sideways, big end that way." She pointed.

He set it inside.

"The other should nestle with the sunburst part in the space that's—"

It was clear, he was way ahead of her, and he set the second one down. They fit perfectly, and he stepped back.

"We're going to have to restrain ourselves for the rest of the afternoon," he said.

"I thought we were done."

"We only made it halfway through the art fair."

"Don't you have to get back to work?"

It was pretty obvious he had problems to solve.

"We've got some time." He shut the lid of the trunk. "I wanted to buy you a painting, or a vase, or maybe some earrings."

Her fingertips rose reflexively to her earlobe. "You can't buy me jewelry on our second date."

He stepped closer. "Why not?"

"It's too…too…" She struggled for the right word. "Intimate."

He took one of her hands, twining his fingers with hers, pulling her closer, his voice going low. "Too intimate? You were there last night, right?"

"That's not the same thing."

"Physical intimacy is not the same as emotional intimacy?"

"It's not." It wasn't.

He gave her what looked like a tolerant smile. "Okay."

"I'll take a vase," she said.

"Sure." He stepped closer, brushing up against her. "Unless you happen to fall madly in love with a pair of earrings."

His touch brought back memories of last night, and fresh desire swept through her. "I won't."

He gave her a warm smile. "Never say never."

She waited for his kiss, eyes closing, lips parting, her chin tipping toward him.

He didn't disappoint.

His lips were hot, his kiss thorough, and his arms wound tight around her. She wished they weren't on a public street. She wished they were back at the inn, wrapped in the cocoon of that soft bed. She desperately wished she could rewind and have last night start all over again.

Riley spoke to Ashton across a hewn wood table at The Copper Tavern. Rock music came from the speaker above them, while a muted Cubs game played out on the screen above the bar.

"We can have the engine mounting bracket custom made," said Riley. "But it's going to be tough on the bottom line. It's a structural part, so we'll need permits and certification. And if he does something like that again, it could sink us."

"Can you stop him?" asked Ashton, as the waitress set two frosted mugs of beer in front of them.

"We're going through the E-22 specs part by part to see where we're vulnerable."

"Can you retaliate? Buy up all the stock of something he needs?"

"His pockets are way deeper than mine," said Riley.

He was ticked off at Shane, but he had to reluctantly admire the play. Now he needed a play of his own.

"What about the girl?" asked Ashton.

"The girl?"

"The twin. Can you use her against Shane?"

"You mean Kalissa?"

"Yeah. Is there a way to parlay that into something—"

"I'm not dragging Kalissa into this." She wasn't a pawn in their battle.

Ashton drew back. "I don't get it. I thought that's why you were dating her."

"That's not why I'm dating her."

"Then why are you dating your rival half-brother's sister-in-law?"

"I like her."

"Sure," Ashton said with a shrug. "I've seen pictures. What's not to like?"

"I mean, I like her. I'm not going to use her to get to Shane."

Ashton stared at him in obvious confusion. "You can't truly fall for Darci's sister."

"I'm not falling for her." But even Riley could hear the lie in that statement.

"I'm serious," said Ashton.

"I've seen her a couple of times, a couple of dates."

Ashton's eyes narrowed further. "And, have you…"

"None of your business."

"Oh, this is great." Ashton threw up his hands. "You're sleeping with her, and you don't want me to know about it?"

"It's none of your—"

"Yeah, yeah. I get it. And when was the last time you were discreet about your sex life?"

Never, was the last time Riley had kept his sex life secret from Ashton. It had never much mattered. It had always been casual, a fleeting good time with women who made no bones about telling their own friends about him.

Riley took a swig of his beer. It was satisfying going down. Though he now wished he had something stronger. He probably should have gone with a boilermaker.

"You can't think this is going to work," said Ashton.

"I don't expect anything to work. I know exactly what's going to happen."

"What's that?"

"As soon as Shane hears my name, he's going to out me as his rival, then he's going to undermine me, and then Kalissa's going to walk away."

Ashton was nodding. "At least it won't come as a surprise."

"It won't come as a surprise. I can handle it."

A beat went past in silence.

"Why don't I believe you?" asked Ashton.

"Because I'm lying." Riley signaled the waitress for a shot.

Ashton held up two fingers. "To me or to yourself?"

"To both of us. I spent half the night trying to figure out a way this doesn't blow up in my face. I mean, why can't I have a chance? Why is it automatically impossible that this gorgeous, bright, enchanting woman can be mine?"

"Do you need an answer to that question?"

"No," said Riley. "I need a plan."

"That's a whole lot harder than an answer."

"Isn't it?"

The waitress dropped off two shots of whiskey.

Both men downed them and took long swallows of their beer.

"You have to tell her," said Ashton.

"I know." That was the only part of the plan that was clear to Riley.

"Before he tells her."

"He doesn't know I'm seeing her."

"He will."

"He will," Riley agreed. "I was thinking one more date. We've had two, three if you count Monday. And they went great. It all went great."

"So, be honest with her."

"I need a little bit more, first." Riley made a space with his finger and thumb. "One more date. If she knows me better, she'll have some perspective. Maybe, just maybe, she'll question some of the negative things he'll tell her."

Ashton gave a sarcastic chuckle. "You really are cynical."

"I prefer to think of it as realistic."

The Cubs hit a two run homer to take the lead in the bottom of the eight, and a cheer went up in the bar.

"I wish I could stay and help you," Ashton said as the noise died down.

The words surprised Riley. "You going somewhere?"

Ashton nodded, his attention on his glass. "I took a search and rescue job in Alaska."

"You *what*?"

"I gotta get away for a while."

Riley was astonished. "From what? Sunshine and civilization?"

Ashton looked up. "I told you about Jennifer."

"Jennifer? You mean the woman who was once Darci's roommate?"

"I need to clear my head."

"You said you two broke up."

"She dumped me."

"So?"

Ashton normally went through multiple girlfriends a

month. Sometimes he walked away, sometimes they did. In the past, it had never bothered him which way it went.

"I don't get the connection to Alaska," said Riley.

"I keep wanting to call her." Ashton signaled for another round of shots.

"So, call her," There was no harm in trying.

"She was pretty definitive last time we talked."

"So instead you want to forget her." Riley thought he got the logic. "I doubt there are a lot of women in Alaska to help with that. Maybe try California."

Ashton chuckled. "I wish it were that easy. I don't want another woman."

"You don't?"

"I haven't been with anyone since Jennifer." Ashton spun his mug. "That was five months ago."

Riley's jaw went lax. "Say, what?"

"I need to clear my head. I don't exactly know what the deal is. I mean, she's great." Ashton paused. "I guess that's it. She's great. Full stop. And I blew it. And I need to get her out of my head before I can move on."

The waitress breezed over with their shots, setting them efficiently on the table. She seemed to gauge the mood of the table and didn't linger for any chit-chat.

"Why didn't you say something?" Riley asked Ashton.

He could have helped. At least, he thought he could have helped. He'd have tried, even though he wasn't exactly a relationship expert.

"I thought I could walk it off. I *am* going to walk it off. But not here. Not in Chicago."

"Is there anything I can do?"

Ashton held up his shot in a toast.

Riley followed suit.

They clicked the glasses together and downed the whisky.

"Don't fall for Kalissa," said Ashton. "It's not going to end well."

"Gotcha." But Riley knew that train was already barreling out of the station.

"Tell her the truth," said Ashton.

"I will."

"I mean now. Right now. Women need to trust you. If Shane beats you to it, you won't be able to dial it back."

Kalissa had lingered in Riley's yard after work was done on Tuesday, but by eight o'clock, he still hadn't come home. She'd told herself he was obviously dealing with his business problems. She mostly believed herself, but she couldn't quite banish the worry that he'd purposely stayed away.

On Wednesday, she was needed on another job site. She briefly considered making an excuse to go to Riley's again, hoping to run into him, but, thankfully, reason overrode emotion. She wasn't going to go chasing after him as if they were in high school.

She spent the day in Oak Park. It was a big, Tudor style house with peaked roof lines and stone facings. The front yard was sleek and modern. It was a corner lot with a three foot stone retaining wall. The owners wanted the front gardens expanded and the yard re-turfed.

By contrast, the backyard was a traditional English garden. It was terribly overgrown, but it had enormous potential, and they'd be working there with plants that were exotic in Chicago.

It's where Kalissa had focused for the day, wandering through trellises and stepping stones, a burbling pond, creeping vines and a profusion of wildflowers.

She heard her name called and popped her head up from a bed of lavender. The sound was coming from the driveway gate.

"Hello?" she called back.

"Kalissa?"

She recognized her sister's voice. She rose to her feet, peeling off her gloves, delighted with the surprise.

"Hey, Darci. What are you doing here?"

"Right now, I'm trying to find you."

"It's a bit overgrown. Follow the sound of my voice."

"I'm trying."

"Can you see the pond?" Kalissa asked. "The stone pathway leads you right there."

"Oh, yes. Here I am, at the pond."

"Take the right hand path. I'll meet you."

"Got it. Shane," Darci called out. "Take a right at the pond."

"What pond?" came Shane's voice from a greater distance.

Darci came into view, and the two women met under a vine covered pergola that shaded them from the sun.

"This is amazing," said Darci, looking around.

"Don't you love it?"

"I want one."

"Maybe for your birthday," Shane joked, emerging along the path.

"It's charming," said Darci.

"Can you build us one of these?" Shane asked Kalissa.

"Sure," Kalissa joked in return. "Just let me know where on your hundred acres you'd like me to put it."

"Anywhere you want," said Shane. "My mother was very particular about the grounds. Me, not so much. You can do whatever you like."

"You should," said Darci, enthusiasm in her voice. "You should re-do the whole place."

Kalissa laughed. "That would take a few years."

Shane shrugged. "It's a good idea."

Kalissa waved him off. "Right."

"I'm serious," he said, looking like he was. "Take over the grounds."

She felt the need to inject some reality into the conversation. "It would be a full time job."

"For more than one person," he said. "How do you think Megan would feel about it?"

"We are not having this conversation," said Kalissa.

"It's not the most outlandish idea in the world," said Darci. "Your work is terrific. And you'd never have to worry about advertising, finding new clients, dealing with difficult people."

"You're not riding in here on your white, billionaire charger and plucking me out of poverty."

"You're in poverty?" asked Shane.

"I'm exaggerating for effect," said Kalissa. Though compared to them, she was certainly impoverished.

She hadn't told them she and Megan lived above the landscaping shop. She'd feared they'd feel compelled to save her from her frugal circumstances.

"Give it some thought," said Shane. "The offer's out there."

"Sure," Kalissa lied. "I'll think about it."

Shane looked at Darci. "She's not going to think about it."

"She might," said Darci.

"She's too proud. Not that I blame her."

"You two can see me standing here, right?" Kalissa laughed.

"You're going to have to get used to us," said Shane.

"I'm trying," she answered honestly. "But I need to manage my own life."

"I understand," said Shane. "And I admire you for it. But at some point, it gets ridiculous."

Kalissa felt her guard go up. "Earning my own living is not ridiculous."

"You're Darci's sister, Ian's daughter, he—"

"Shane," Darci's tone was unusually sharp. "It can wait."

"It can," Shane agree. "I apologize, Kalissa." He glanced around the yard. "Why don't you tell us what you're doing here?"

Kalissa knew they hadn't stopped by to hear about her landscaping job. "What's going on?" she asked her sister.

"I really want to hear about the garden," said Darci.

"No, you don't."

"Yes, I do."

"You two sound like a couple of eight year olds," said Shane, a trace of laughter in his voice.

"That's because we missed being eight year olds together," said Darci. "Tell me," she said to Kalissa.

Kalissa gave in. "We'll have to cut a lot of it back, and re-do a bunch of the woodwork. You saw the pond? We're going to expand it and create a recirculating creak, with a little waterfall to aerate it. I love the wildflowers. They attract dragonflies, bumble bees, butterflies. When we're—"

A figure appeared in Kalissa's peripheral vision, standing at the edge of the pergola, silhouetted against the sun.

Kalissa shaded her eyes to see. "Riley?"

A glow of pleasure grew in her chest. She was frighteningly glad to see him.

"Hi, Kalissa." His tone was soft, intimate, his focus intent on her. "Megan said you'd be here."

Shane swiftly looked over his shoulder. "*Ellis*?" His voice was incredulous.

Riley's expression froze, his gaze darting to Shane and sticking.

"What are you doing here?" Shane demanded.

Kalissa's chest went hollow. "You two know each other?"

"Yes, I know him," said Shane, turning fully and planting his feet apart. "He's Ellis Aviation, the guy who's been a thorn in my side."

Kalissa didn't understand. "Riley?"

"I need to talk to you," Riley said to Kalissa.

Kalissa took in Darci's tense expression. "What's going on?"

"He's not a good man," Darci said to Kalissa. She looked quite upset.

"He's the scheming competition," Shane barked. "Tell me how you know him."

Kalissa recoiled from the anger in Shane's voice. "We met a couple of weeks ago."

She scrambled her thoughts back to the restaurant that night, trying to remember how it had played out. Riley had though she was Darci. And he'd confronted her, accused her of spying on him.

"By chance," said Riley.

"I just bet it was," said Shane. He shifted, putting himself between Kalissa and Riley.

"We need to talk," Riley said to Kalissa, moving so he could see her.

"I don't think so," said Shane.

"You knew them," she said to Riley, assailed by a feeling of betrayal. "You knew them all along."

"Not the way you think," said Riley.

"What way do I think?"

No wonder Shane was angry. Riley had played her, and she'd fallen for it hook, line and sinker. She'd dated him. She'd slept with him.

"What did you tell him?" asked Shane, his voice bitter.

She hadn't told him anything. What could she tell him? She didn't know anything.

"Leave her alone," demanded Riley.

Darci moved closer to Kalissa, linking their arms.

"*Me* leave her alone?" Shane spat out.

"It's not her fault," said Riley.

Shane's voice lowered, sounding more controlled. "What's your game?"

"*My* game?" Riley scoffed.

Kalissa's throat went tight. She felt a tremor start deep inside her. She couldn't listen to this. She couldn't stand to know she might have compromised Darci and Shane.

Riley had pretended to like her in a bid to undermine her family. Mortification washed over her as she remembered the things they'd done together.

"Do you want to get out of here?" Darci whispered in her ear.

Kalissa gave a jerky nod.

"Let's go." Darci urged her to the side of the pergola, skirting Riley.

"Don't go," he called to her.

"Who *are* you?" she managed, her voice quaking. "Why would you *do* that to me?"

"I came to tell you," he said. "The reason I'm here right now is to tell you the truth."

"You expect me to believe that?" She was through being naive.

"Don't talk to her," said Shane. "Talk to me."

Riley shot him a glare.

Darci urged her forward, and Kalissa went willingly.

Seven

Riley moved to go after Kalissa, but Shane was on him in a second, blocking his path.

"Don't talk to her," Shane growled. "Don't touch her. Don't go near her *ever* again."

"Back off," said Riley, voice tight, sorely tempted to take a swing.

"No, you back off, you son-of-a-bitch."

Riley saw red. He stepped up, only inches from Shane's face. "Are you *out of your mind?* My mother was one of the sweetest, most gentle, hardest working people who ever lived. I don't give a damn what you say to me or about me, but don't you ever, dare—"

"Whoa," Shane drew back, looking shocked. "It's an expression."

"Yeah, right," Riley spat with disgust. "It's just an expression."

"It is."

"Nothing to do with you and me."

It shouldn't have surprised Riley that Shane was feigning ignorance of their relationship. It was all he'd ever done.

Shane's expression hardened again. "*Kalissa* is what has to do with you and me."

Riley's anger warred with regret. He didn't want to cause her any grief. "She didn't tell me a thing. She didn't have to. Your moves are pretty obvious."

"My moves? *My* moves?"

"The engine mounting bracket."

"What engine mounting bracket?"

"You're going to lie about it, too? Come on, Colborn, at least be man enough to admit it when you undermine me."

Shane looked confused. "You're the one who headhunted my guys."

"I did that. And I was up front about it."

"You failed."

"I got a couple of them," said Riley.

"Not the best."

"Not yet."

Shane's tone seemed to moderate. "You're still trying to sink me?"

"You're trying to sink me. Every Bradley lower front engine mounting bracket from every distributor? Not a lot of finesse to that move."

"Somebody bought up *just* the lower fronts?"

"Yeah, you did."

"It wasn't me."

Shane looked so sincere that it gave Riley pause.

"Are you that good at lying?" asked Riley.

"What would be the point of lying?"

"That's what I'm trying to figure out." Riley knew it was going to be fairly easy to confirm.

Shane drew an exasperated sigh. "Stay away from Kalissa. She's got nothing to do with this."

"Agreed." Riley didn't want Kalissa to have anything to do with the feud between him and Shane. "But I'm not staying away from her."

"Oh, yes you are."

Riley sputtered a ragged laugh. "Not happening."

Anger flooded back into Shane's eyes. "Are you looking for a fight?"

"No. But I'm not backing down from one either."

Shane would try to sway Kalissa. Riley couldn't stop that. But he had a side to this story, too.

He wasn't going to tuck his tail between his legs and walk away from what he wanted because his golden-child half-brother demanded it.

Not this time.

"I can protect her," said Shane.

"You don't have to protect her. Not from me." Something

compelled Riley to be honest. "I'm not going to do a thing to hurt her."

"You already have."

"I wish I hadn't. That wasn't my intent. When I take you on, Shane, I'll do it straight up. I'm not hiding behind a woman."

"Again, you already have."

"I was trying to figure out how to tell her."

"That you were plotting against her family? Yeah, I can see how that's a hard subject to bring up."

Riley had been trying to figure out how to tell Kalissa that Shane was his *brother.* There was a root cause to this bad blood. Could they not at least be upfront about that when they were alone?

What exactly was Shane's problem? Was he afraid he was being quoted or recorded, that Riley would defame their father's name or go after the inheritance? Did he resent Riley so much that he couldn't even bring himself to say the words?

Riley knew it was probably all of that.

"This conversation is pointless," he said. He turned to walk away.

He made it only a few steps.

"Was it working?" Shane asked from behind.

Riley stopped. "Was what working?"

"Were you getting to her?"

Riley considered his answer. He turned back. "She likes me."

Shane scowled at him, jaw set. "You hurt her, and I'll annihilate you."

"You're already trying to annihilate me. But my beef is with you. I won't use her as a pawn."

This time, Riley did walk away, out of the yard and around the big house.

He slammed the door of his car and peeled away from the curb, bringing up the revs and increasing his speed until a traffic light forced him to brake. Then he smacked his hand down on the steering wheel.

He didn't doubt for a second that Shane would protect

Kalissa. He had the resources to put an impenetrable wall around her.

Riley had to talk to her. He had to convince her that what they'd shared was real. Yes, he'd stayed silent about Shane. But it wasn't so he could use her. It was so she'd give them a chance to get to know each other.

A chance was all he'd wanted, all he still wanted. A chance to hear the sound of her voice, feel the silk of her skin, and taste the sweetness of her lips all over again.

The driver behind him honked his horn, and Riley hit the gas.

Kalissa was *not* going to dissolve into a puddle of emotion.

"It's no big deal," she said to Darci across the table in the garden tearoom.

Barely five blocks from the Oak Park house, her sister had directed her into a restaurant parking lot. The place was unnaturally serene, with piped flute music, a burbling fountain, white wrought iron furniture and dozens if not hundreds of potted plants decorating the terra cotta brick floor.

"We only met a couple of weeks ago," she said.

Darci waited, and Kalissa recognized the technique.

It was one she used herself when one of her friends was upset. Let them talk their way through it and get it straight in their own head before you offered any advice.

"I know what you're doing," she said to Darci.

Darci smiled. "What am I doing?"

"You're letting me think this through."

"Is that a bad thing?"

"No, it's a strange thing. It's what I usually do with other people."

"Are you getting anywhere?" asked Darci.

"Not really. I wish I was. I mean, he seemed so great. Yeah, it was weird when we first met. He actually thought I was you. And he accused me of spying on him. I guess I pushed the significance of that to the side when I started to like him. I told myself he must have seen your picture in the media, because he said he'd never met you."

"He hasn't."

"But he knows Shane."

"Not really. He's Shane's competition, but I don't think they'd met in person."

Kalissa digested the information. "At least he wasn't lying. Well, about that much, anyway."

The waitress brought them hot tea and scones. Kalissa would have preferred something stronger than Earl Gray, but she didn't want to seem crass.

"Did he lie about other things?" asked Darci, spooning sugar into her tea.

"There's no way to know. Man, it felt like such a whirlwind. I thought…I mean…Okay, this is so embarrassing."

Darci reached out and touched her hand. "We're sisters."

Some of the tension eased in Kalissa. "We are. Not that I know how to be a sister."

"We'll make it up as we go along."

"We can, can't we? It's not like you'll be able to call me on doing it wrong."

Darci smiled into her cup.

Kalissa braced herself, rotating her own cup in its delicate saucer. "I thought I finally knew what it was like to be falling in love. There. I said it. I feel like an idiot."

"I'm so sorry," said Darci.

"It's not your fault."

"For any part Shane's relationship with Riley might have played in messing this up."

"It was messed up to start with. Shane was the only reason Riley gave me a second look."

"I don't believe that for a second." Darci gave a small laugh. "It's weird, trying to compliment someone who looks exactly like you. I was about to tell you, you were beautiful. But that's like complimenting myself."

"You *are* beautiful," said Kalissa.

"Shane thinks so. So, we've got him on our side."

"I read that he was named the most eligible bachelor in Chicago."

"And *he* picked *us*."

"He picked *you*." Kalissa sobered. "You don't suppose the two of them are fighting back there?"

"Maybe," said Darci.

"I meant a fistfight. They both seemed really upset. Maybe we shouldn't have left."

"Quick, gut reaction, don't think about it, who do you want to win?"

Riley.

Kalissa closed her eyes and a sense of longing overwhelmed her. She missed him. She'd started missing him the minute he dropped her off on Monday night.

She'd been so ridiculously happy to see him today. In the split second before Shane had spoken, she'd already imagined Riley's arms around her, holding her tight against his strong body. It had felt so, so good.

"I slept with him," she blurted out.

Darci's brow went up.

"In Lake Forest. We had dinner at this cute little inn. Then we got a room. It was fantastic. Best sex I've ever had."

Darci's mouth twitched in a smile. "Wow. I like being sisters." Then, she grew serious. "I mean, oh, I'm so sorry."

"I don't usually do it that fast. That is…" Kalissa groaned. "I feel like I should defend my morals. I don't sleep around."

"Good to know. Not that I care. I slept with Shane while I was spying on him. That's not exactly admirable."

"You spied on Shane?"

"Long story. I'll tell you about it sometime." Darci tore off a bite of her scone.

"Thank you," Kalissa said softly. "For being here and listening."

"I'm sorry you got hurt."

"I'll get over it." Kalissa hoped this annoying, empty ache would disappear soon. "Darci, he was so good at seduction. I bought into everything he said."

"You weren't expecting him to lie."

"No, I guess not. Did he think I'd have insider information on Colborn Aerospace?"

"You might. You could have. You probably will someday."

"No." Kalissa held up her palm. "You are never, *ever* to tell me anything about Shane's company. Clearly, I'm the weak link."

Darci gave what looked like an amused smile. "We'll see."

"What do you mean, we'll see. Just agree to keep quiet."

"You might need to know someday. And what are the odds someone else will target you to get to Colborn?"

"Small, I suppose." Kalissa's thoughts returned to Riley.

"Zero," said Darci.

"Do you suppose he wanted something specific?"

"He's been undercutting Shane on international contracts. And he tried to hire away some of the Colborn staff."

"He didn't seem underhanded." She sipped her tea and discovered it was now lukewarm. "Then again, I guess he showed me what he wanted me to see."

"A harmless, trustworthy guy."

Memories were coming back to Kalissa. "It took him the longest time to give me his last name. For a while there, I thought he was in the witness protection program, because something seemed off. He told me he was a conspiracy theorist, but it didn't ring true. Then again, I suppose he was the one plotting the conspiracy. And he really downplayed his business. Though, I guess telling me the details would give away his secret. He made it sound small, nothing like Colborn."

"It's a lot smaller than Colborn," said Darci.

"He's ambitious," said Kalissa, guessing he must be jealous of Shane's success.

"He's ruthless and scheming."

Kalissa agreed.

He was also sexy and witty, astute and charming. But she had to forget those qualities. If she didn't, it would be impossible to forget him.

* * *

Riley hated approaching Kalissa out on the street, but he couldn't take the chance of waiting until tomorrow. Shane was sure to put some kind of protection around her. He might even move her behind the walls of his mansion.

Riley was certain she'd never show up at his house to work again. He expected Mosaic to simply walk away from the job, leaving his yard half done.

So he was waiting in the alcove next to the Mosaic shop, under an awning to keep out of the drizzling rain. Megan had gone inside about an hour ago. But she'd been walking, and their pickup wasn't parked out front, so Riley had hope that he hadn't missed Kalissa.

He still wasn't sure what he was going to say. Apologize, sure. But he also had to convince her to give him another chance. He knew it was a long shot, but he had to take it.

A pair of headlights rounded the corner, the beams flashing off the dim building of the narrow street. Water splashed beneath the tires. It was a pickup, and it was the right color.

It pulled into a vacant spot. The driver's door opened, and he tensed as he recognized her, auburn hair cascading forward as she climbed out. He gazed at her slim shoulders and long legs, that pretty profile he'd watched so many times.

She slung a big purse over her shoulder. Then she locked the door and scooted across the street, avoiding puddles along the way.

"Kalissa?" He wanted her to hear his voice and know it was him before she saw a man lurking in the shadows.

She stopped five feet from the curb.

"It's Riley," he said.

She glanced up and down the darkened street. "What are you doing here?"

"I need to talk to you."

"I have nothing to say."

"Please just listen."

She walked determinedly forward. "No."

"Kalissa."

She halted beside him. "What? You're going to tell me some more lies?"

"I want to explain."

"That's pointless. I don't trust you."

"I understand."

Her tone dripped with sarcasm. "How magnanimous of you, to understand why I might not trust a lying jerk who lured me into his bed."

"I didn't—"

"Come on, Riley. You're going to tell me you didn't have sex with me?"

"I meant I didn't lure you."

She lifted her chin. "You're right. I came willingly. What's your point?"

"My point is I'm sorry."

Her voice was brittle. "For having sex with me?"

"No. *No. Never.* I'd have sex with you a thousand times more." He knew the words were wrong, but he couldn't seem to stop them. "I wanted to tell you about Ellis Aviation, about Shane, about everything."

"What stopped you?"

"I knew you'd walk away."

"I *would* have walked away."

"And I didn't want that. You meant too much to me. You *mean* too much to me."

"I meant nothing to you."

The light rain was dampening her hair, glistening when it misted her cheeks.

He reached for her hand, but she jerked it away, hiding it behind her back.

"If you meant nothing to me," he said. "I wouldn't be here."

Instead of responding, she clamped her jaw shut.

"Think about it, Kalissa. My cover's blown. From a business perspective, I'm sunk. There's only one reason for me to be here."

She seemed to ponder his words for a few moments. Then

she spoke. "Just because I can't see the scheme, doesn't mean you're not hatching one."

"Sometimes it does."

"You're too smart for me, Riley. You know things I don't know. You want things I can't understand."

"I want you."

She shook her head. "You already played that card."

"It wasn't a game. Everything between us was true."

"You mean there were no other lies? Only the ones I caught you in? Do I look stupid? Do I act stupid?"

He battled an urge to reach for her. "I was going to tell you. I was trying to figure out the right time and the right way."

"I don't believe that for a second."

"I thought if you got to know me, if I could make you like me, if I had a chance before Shane turned you against me, you might listen to my side of the story."

"You can't make me trust you by lying to me."

Ashton's words echoed inside Riley's head.

"I know that. If I could go back, I'd have told you that first day." He hesitated. "Maybe."

She folded her arms across her chest and pursed her lips with obvious impatience.

"I'm trying to be honest here," he said. "If I could go back, it would be hard. If I told you up front, you'd have never agreed to go out with me."

She gave a sharp nod of agreement.

"And we wouldn't have had that night on the pier, or that drive up the coast, or the night in—"

"Stop it, Riley."

"I can't stop thinking about it."

"You have to stop thinking about it."

"Can you?"

Her slight hesitation told him there was a chance. A very, very small chance he could get through to her.

"Yes," she said in a small voice.

"Now who's lying?"

She opened her mouth.

He reached out and put his finger across it. "Don't lie to me, Kalissa. I've done enough of that for the both of us."

He couldn't stop himself. He stepped forward.

"I can't," she said, a catch in her voice.

"I'm not asking you to trust me."

Her eyes were wide and luminous in the pale streetlights. She looked frightened and uncertain. He hated himself for doing that to her.

"All I ask is a chance," he said, struggling to control his own emotions. "Don't walk away."

She blinked rapidly, and he drew her into his arms.

"I'm so sorry, Kalissa. I'd give anything to start over, to make circumstances different."

Her voice was muffled against him. "We can't."

"I want to figure this out."

"She's my sister, Riley." But her body had molded against his.

"I know."

"I've only just found her."

"I know that too." He tightened his hold.

"You're trying to harm them."

He wasn't. Then again, he was. He was trying to harm Colborn Aerospace. "That has nothing to do with you."

She drew back to look up at him. "You can't put me in the middle."

"I won't," he pledged.

"You are."

"Kalissa." He brought his palm to her cheek.

Her skin was so smooth, so soft, warming beneath his touch.

His gaze moved to her lips.

It might be the last time. He couldn't let it be the last time. He simply couldn't let this be the last time he kissed her.

He brought his mouth to hers, and he pulled her tight. Her lips were hot and soft and sweet. They parted beneath his, and he kissed her deeply, arousal coming to life within him.

He longed to be back in Lake Forest. He wished they'd never come home.

"Ms. Smith?" came a deep officious male voice.

Footsteps beat toward them.

Kalissa jerked back, obviously alarmed.

"Don't worry," said Riley, knowing exactly what was going on. "He'll be from Shane."

Riley straightened to glare at the man, keeping one arm around Kalissa. "Are you trying to scare her to death?"

"I'm paid to protect her."

Kalissa turned to the tall, angular man. "Protect me from what? Who are you?"

"Your brother-in-law Shane Colborn asked me to make sure you're safe at all times." The man eyed Riley up and down.

"No way," said Kalissa.

"She doesn't want you around," said Riley.

"My name is Patrick Garrison, ma'am. I'm with West Shore Security Services."

Kalissa retrieved her phone. "Please tell me you're not armed."

"You don't need to worry about that, ma'am."

She dialed her phone.

Riley met the man's steady gaze. He got that the guy was a professional bodyguard, but he wasn't about to be intimidated.

"Darci?" said Kalissa. "I'm standing outside my apartment looking at a guy from West Shore Security."

She glanced at Riley.

"I don't think he would," she said into the phone.

Patrick Garrison's phone rang.

He answered. "Yes, sir?" There was a pause. "She is." Another pause, and Garrison's gaze went to Riley. "I'm assuming it's him."

"It's me," said Riley.

"This is ludicrous," Kalissa said to Darci.

"I will, sir," said Garrison. "Absolutely." He ended the call.

Riley's phone rang.

Kalissa carried on with Darci. "Tell Shane to, I don't know, fire him, I guess."

Garrison smirked.

Riley checked the screen on his phone. The number was blocked.

He put it to his ear. "Yeah?"

"It's Shane."

"No kidding."

"What are you doing?"

"I'm talking to Kalissa. What are *you* doing?"

"I'm protecting Kalissa."

"So am I," said Riley.

"From you."

"She doesn't need it. She doesn't want it."

Kalissa was gaping at Riley while she spoke to Darci. "Tell me that's not Shane talking to Riley."

Riley gave her a nod of affirmation.

"*Darci.*"

Garrison stepped back, and Riley could swear he looked amused.

Kalissa held up a hand. "This is *ludicrous*!"

"Tell her to come stay with us," said Shane.

"I'm not going to—" But then Riley realized Shane was talking to Darci.

"Don't to it," Riley said to Kalissa.

"What?" Kalissa said into the phone. "No." Her gaze darted to Garrison. "I'm sure he will, but—"

"She's staying here," Riley said to Shane.

"It's none of your business," replied Shane.

"Riley's not going to hurt me," Kalissa insisted.

"They think I'll *hurt* you?" Riley couldn't believe they'd even suggest it. "Quit messing with her mind," he said to Shane.

"No," Kalissa repeated into the phone.

"What are you saying to her?" Riley asked Shane. He immediately realized it was a stupid question. "What are they saying?" he asked Kalissa instead.

"They want me to have Garrison drive me to the mansion."

"You already told them no." Then Riley looked at his phone and realized he didn't need to be talking to Shane. He hung up.

"We need to talk," he told Kalissa with conviction. Then he glared at Garrison. "She's perfectly safe."

The man crossed his arms over his chest. "Oh, I know she's going to be safe."

"Say goodbye to Darci," said Riley.

"I have to go," Kalissa said into the phone. "I have to talk to Riley." She paused. "Five minutes." She silently nodded. "I will. Bye."

Thankfully, she ended the call.

"Back off," Riley said to Garrison.

Garrison looked to Kalissa.

"This is foolish," she said.

"No argument from me, ma'am."

"Can you." She made a shooing motion with her hands. "Just back off a bit?"

"Whatever you say, ma'am."

"Clearly, that's not going to be the case," Kalissa mumbled.

Despite everything, Riley's mouth twitched at the comical situation.

"You think this is funny?" she demanded.

"No. Sorry."

"It's not funny."

"I know."

"Stop laughing."

"I did."

She stared at him, her chest rising and falling with deep breaths.

"Can we talk?" he asked, sobering completely. "Just the two of us? Somewhere...not here?"

She didn't answer. Uncertainty flicked through her beautiful eyes.

He knew he had to convince her. "We need to talk."

"I can't trust you."

"I know. I understand. But you were there, Kalissa. This isn't nothing. We can't just walk away."

She still didn't answer.

He reached out and took her hand.

She looked down. It took her a long time to speak. "It can't be tonight."

He was disappointed in that, but he could live with it. "When?"

"Can I call you?"

"*Will* you call me?"

She frowned.

"If you don't, I'm calling you."

She squeezed her eyes shut. "Okay."

He eased in. "I want to kiss you."

"You can't."

"I want it bad."

She opened her eyes. "Garrison might shoot you."

"He won't risk hitting you."

"I think he's probably a good shot."

Garrison was likely an excellent shot. Riley couldn't imagine Shane hiring anyone but the best.

But he didn't want to kiss her in front of her bodyguard. He wanted to kiss her all alone, preferably in a bedroom, his bedroom. He bit back a curse.

"I'll miss you every second," he told her instead.

"I'm not making any promises."

"I know."

He had to accept her hesitation. He had a long way to go before she'd trust him again. And Shane would be working against him. Shane would do everything in his power to make sure Riley failed.

Eight

In the morning, Patrick Garrison was waiting on the sidewalk outside Mosaic Landscaping.

Kalissa's surprise was quickly overtaken by concern. "Please tell me you haven't been here all night."

"Hello?" said Megan. "This is the guy?"

"This is the guy," said Kalissa. "Did you stay here?" she asked Garrison.

"I'm Megan." Megan held out her hand.

"I just came on shift, ma'am," Garrison said to Kalissa, briefly shaking Megan's hand.

"Ma'am?" asked Megan. "He calls you ma'am."

"For some reason," said Kalissa. "So, how does this work? Are you actually planning to follow me around all day long?"

There was the faintest of smirks on Garrison's face. "It helps if I stay close to you."

"You know this is unnecessary, right?" She realized he was being paid by Shane, and he had to do his job, but he had to have seen last night that Riley was no real threat.

She couldn't figure out Riley's angle. It was pretty obvious he'd romanced her in the hope she'd get him information on Colborn Aerospace. But he was caught now, so there was no way that was ever happening.

So, why did he persist? Why the pretty words last night? And why had she, even for a moment, considered he might be sincere?

"You're actually her bodyguard," said Megan, peering at Garrison as if he was from another planet.

Garrison stared back, his expression inscrutable. He didn't answer.

"Are you armed?" asked Megan.

"He doesn't like to talk about that," said Kalissa. "Should I drive slow so you can keep up?"

Garrison's smirk was back. "Not necessary. But it'll be easier if you ride with me."

Megan's expression brightened. "Like our chauffer?"

Garrison frowned at her. "I was referring to Ms. Smith."

Megan linked her arm with Kalissa's. "I'm with her. You can drive us both."

"He's not driving us anywhere."

Kalissa could put up with Garrison following her around. He seemed quiet and well-behaved. She didn't think he'd get in the way. And, quite frankly, she didn't have the energy to fight Shane. She needed all her brain power to work through the situation with Riley.

"We can stop for canned pomerinis on the way home," said Megan. "He'd be our designated driver."

"Canned pomerinis?" asked Garrison.

"Pomegranate and candy apple martinis," said Megan.

Garrison shuddered. "Is that a joke?"

Kalissa started for their pickup truck. "I'll try not to lose you," she said.

Garrison immediately turned his back on Megan and fell into step beside Kalissa. "I'd prefer it if you'd come with me," he said.

"We need the tools in the back of the truck."

"I can drive the truck."

"The gearshift is a bit tricky."

He stifled a cough. "I think I can manage."

"Oh, let him drive," said Megan. "I was serious about the canned pomerinis."

"I wouldn't advise excessive amounts of alcohol," said Garrison, stopping as Kalissa stopped next to the truck.

"You're not going to be a buzz kill, are you?" asked Megan.

Garrison looked down at her. "Do you *have* to be part of this conversation?"

"Hey, buddy. I'm on your side."

Megan raised a playful fist to sock him on the arm. Kalissa had seen her do it a thousand times.

Garrison's hand moved like lightning, grabbing her wrist.

"Whoa," said Megan, taking a half step back.

"That was impressive," said Kalissa.

Garrison immediately let Megan go. "I'm not trying to be impressive. I'm just trying to do my job." His attention was on Kalissa. "And that job will be a whole lot easier if you let me drive. So, what do you say?"

Since it was by far the longest speech she'd heard him make, she decided to take it seriously.

She had no reason to make Garrison's life difficult. She could argue this out with Shane, or she could make the best of it. A couple of days, a week max, it should all blow over. Riley would give up, Shane would stop worrying, and Garrison could go back to guarding people who were in some kind of real danger.

"Fine," she agreed, digging into the pocket of her blue jeans. "The brakes are spongy, there's a shudder when you take a hard left, and if you hit a bump, it'll jump out of second."

Megan pulled open the passenger door and climbed to the middle of the bench seat.

Kalissa was happy to take the window.

"I'm calling Riley," she told Garrison as he slammed the driver's door shut. "You might want to get another job lined up, because this'll be over soon."

"To the Oak Park jobsite," said Megan in a theatrical voice. "It's nine-thirty-seven—"

"I know where it is," said Garrison.

"How do you know that?"

He shot Megan a look of disbelief.

"You investigated us?"

Kalissa found Riley's number in her contact list.

"I broke into your computer," said Garrison.

"No way," said Megan.

Kalissa put the phone to her ear.

"Saw everything," said Garrison.

"Not the—" Megan clamped her jaw shut, clearly trying to figure out it Garrison was messing with her.

"Kalissa?" Riley answered.

"Hi," she said, her chest going warm at the sound of his voice.

She angled herself toward the window as the truck gained speed down the street. She realized Garrison could still hear her, but she didn't want him to see her expression on top of everything else.

"How are you?" asked Riley.

"I'm okay." She drew a breath, telling herself to get a grip.

This wasn't a budding romance. It was a failed attempt at espionage. Her next move wasn't to swoon in Riley's arms. It was to convince him she was a lost cause. He'd have to find some other advantage over Shane.

"When can I see you?" he asked.

"The sooner the better."

His voice brightened. "Yeah?"

"Not for that."

"I'm not making any assumptions."

"You said we had to talk."

"We do."

"I agree." She glanced at Megan and Garrison.

Both were silent and focused out the windshield. But she knew they had to be listening to every word. Megan, because she knew Kalissa was still attracted to Riley, and Garrison because he'd want a heads-up regarding her plans.

"I'll come to you," said Riley. "Are you at home?"

"We're on our way to Oak Park."

"We?"

"Me, Megan and Garrison."

Riley chuckled, sounding more amused than worried. "I gotta hand it to Shane."

The words puzzled her. "What do you mean?"

"I'd have done exactly the same thing. If I was him, I wouldn't let you anywhere near me."

"Should I be staying away?"

"No way. I'm not him, I'm me, and I want to get as close to you as possible."

"I don't even know how to take that."

"What's he saying?" asked Garrison.

Kalissa gave the man a warning glare.

"This isn't what you think, Kalissa," said Riley.

"What do I think?"

"I'm heading for the car. I'm on my way. Let's talk when I get there."

"I'm only going to tell you this can't happen." For some reason, her stomach cramped over the words.

"I know that."

"I can't trust you."

"I know that too."

Her mind went to last night, and their kiss, and his words. And she couldn't help having second thoughts about the wisdom of seeing him in person. He seemed to know exactly what to say to throw her off.

There was no possible way this was a coincidence. He was using her, and she needed to end it quickly and completely.

"I'll see you there." She quit the call before he could answer.

"What are you going to say to him?" asked Megan, giving Kalissa's shoulder a rub.

"I'm going to tell him to go away and never bother me again."

"Works for me," said Garrison.

"Works for me too," said Kalissa, mentally crossing her fingers.

She had to stick to her guns. She couldn't let herself get lost in Riley's sexy voice or look too deeply into his dark eyes, because then she'd start wondering, she'd start hoping—

"Do you think there's any chance at all it's a coincidence?" she said out loud.

"No," said Garrison.

"That what's a coincidence?" asked Megan.

"Riley falling for me, me falling for him, completely independent of anything between him and Shane."

"No," Garrison repeated.

"How do you mean?" asked Megan.

Garrison frowned at Megan. "Don't encourage her."

"What encourage her? I'm asking a simple question."

"To which the answer is no. He's Colborn's business rival. He lied about who he was. He romanced and seduced her. That's one impossible coincidence." Garrison downshifted to take a tight corner.

"I'm not saying it was." Megan's voice rose. "I'm just asking what she means." She turned to Kalissa. "What do you mean?"

"I mean…" Kalissa wasn't exactly sure what she meant.

She was grasping at straws. She wanted to believe Riley liked her, that he was attracted to her, that he'd somehow fallen for her in record time. Because the alternative was that he was cruel and she was foolish. She didn't want either of those things to be true.

Riley caught the grim expression on Garrison's face as Kalissa opened the passenger door of his sports car.

"If you get in, it'll give us some privacy," he told her.

She gave a nod of agreement and sat down.

Garrison took a step toward them, then another.

Kalissa shut the door.

Riley gave a half second's hesitation, then he let his instincts kick in. He turned the key, shoved it into first and peeled away from the curb.

"What are you *doing*?" Kalissa demanded.

"Giving us some privacy," he said as he glanced in the rear view mirror.

Garrison was sprinting back to Kalissa's truck, leaping into the driver's seat.

"Riley!"

"Do up your seatbelt."

"Stop."

He swung the sports car around a tight corner, barely slowing for the stop sign. "I can't stop. We need a few minutes alone."

"So, you're *kidnapping* me."

"Technically, yeah, I guess." He glanced in the rear view mirror.

"You *guess*?"

There was no way the pickup truck could outrace him, but he didn't dare hit a stoplight. "I had to get you away from him."

"Why? He was only going to stand there and watch."

A red light loomed up, and Riley switched to the right lane, pausing for a truck to go by before swinging in front of a minivan. The driver hit the horn.

"Riley!"

"I didn't want him to stand there and watch."

"This is dangerous."

"There's nothing to be afraid of."

"You mean, other than death in a fiery crash?"

There was a distinct edge of sarcasm to her tone. He couldn't tell if she was frightened or angry.

"We're not going to crash. I'll slow down in a minute."

He wove his way through traffic, gaining speed on a straight stretch.

Her cell phone rang.

"Damn." He knew there was no way to stop her from answering.

She pulled it out, shaking her head at him in annoyance as she put it to her ear. "Hello?"

She paused a moment. "You don't think I already *told* him to stop?"

"Is it Garrison or Shane," asked Riley, re-evaluating his rash plan.

This may have been a mistake. He could have been more subtle, gaining Kalissa's and maybe even Garrison's trust before trying to get her alone. But he'd known this might be his last chance.

"No," Kalissa said into the phone. "Don't call the police. He's stopping. He told me he'd let me out."

Riley glanced at her in surprise, trying to guess what she was doing, afraid to hope it could be in his favor. But he was too busy driving to look at her for long.

"I'll call you back," she said into the phone. Then she disconnected. "You've got Garrison completely freaked out."

They came up on the river, and he swung off the main road, onto the forest road that he knew led to a small parking lot.

"I swear I just want to talk."

"You think this will make me *listen*?"

"I don't know what I'm thinking," he confessed. "This was spur of the moment."

He slowed the vehicle as they drove into the near empty parking lot. His heart rate calmed and the adrenaline stopped pumping.

"I can't stand the thought of Shane keeping you away from me," he said. "I can't stand it, Kalissa. If it's your choice, fine. If you can't get past my secrets, and you want me gone, I'm gone. But it's not going to be *him*. It's not going to be *his* choice."

He swung into a spot on the far side of a parking lot that bordered an oak and aspen forest. Then he shut off the engine and silence rose around them.

"What do you think you can say that could possibly make a difference?" she asked.

He turned in his seat, struggling to compose something in his mind.

"I can only tell you the truth. And I'll admit it, for a moment, *only* a moment, the day when I called to hire you, I thought about how I could use you against Shane."

"You can't."

"I never tried. It was for a few seconds, max. But then I realized why I was really calling you. I liked you. I was attracted to you. I wanted to get to know you."

"We'd had a five minute conversation on the restaurant patio. And you were mostly yelling at me."

"I know. But there was something there." Again, he searched for the words. "It was an instantaneous attraction."

"How convenient for you."

He'd known this wasn't going to be easy, and he struggled to stay calm. "Did I ask about Shane? In all the time we were together, did I ever once bring up Colborn Aerospace?"

"I'm sure you were leading up to that."

"I wasn't. I knew you'd eventually tell them my name. And I knew when you did all hell would break loose."

"So, why didn't you tell me?"

"I was planning to—"

"I mean, before you slept with me. That would have been a nice thing to do, Riley."

"I didn't plan to sleep with you."

She scoffed out an exclamation of disbelief. "We just happened to have dinner at a romantic little inn up the coast?"

"I didn't even think of that place until we were halfway there. I was winging it at that point."

"And I should believe this, why?"

Her phone rang again.

"Don't answer it."

She lifted the phone. "He'll only zero in on my GPS."

"That's in the movies."

"I think it's real." She raised the phone to her ear.

"I'm fine," she said.

Riley wondered if it was still Garrison, or if Shane had joined the party.

Then she held the phone out to him.

"Which one?" he mouthed.

That earned him a flash of a grin. "It's Garrison."

Riley figured he had little to lose. He accepted the phone. "Yeah?"

Garrison's tone was rigid. "Whatever it is you're doing, stop."

"We're talking."

"Where are you?"

"Yeah, right."

"Listen, I'm the most reasonable guy you get to deal with on this. And if you harm one hair on her head."

"What is *with* that? I don't care what my— I don't care what Shane told you, I am *not* going to hurt Kalissa."

Riley took in her flushed cheeks, her slightly mussed hair, the worn T-shirt and those faded jeans atop well used leather work boots. He'd do anything for her, anything, he realized—including let her go.

He looked straight into her eyes, still talking into the phone. "I've said my piece. I'm done. We're in the river parking lot, across from the pond."

The line went dead.

Kalissa blinked at him in obvious confusion.

He handed back her phone. "There's nothing more I can say. The ball's in your court."

He levered out of the car and walked to the passenger side, opening her door to wait for Garrison.

As she stepped out, he tried to muster up a smile. "I do still want to kiss you."

She was close, just a foot away. The sunshine reflected off her creamy skin and glowed in her deep, green eyes.

"I don't know what to think."

"I can't help you there." He smoothed his palm across her cheek, maybe for the last time. "I know what I think, and I know I'm being honest. But you're going to have to make up your own mind."

He heard a vehicle turn the corner beyond the trees.

Her voice was soft. "I'm scared."

"Don't be scared. It's just a relationship. You can break it off any old time you want."

"I don't want to hurt Darci."

"Do you think Darci wants to hurt you? We can make this work, Kalissa. You and me can just be you and me. We never have to talk about them. We don't even have to mention their names. There's no way for me to use you against Shane if we never even mention their names."

The truck pulled into the parking lot.

She swallowed. She opened her mouth, then she closed it again. "I'll call you."

He gave a self-deprecating smile. "That's what you said last time."

"And, I did."

He had to admit, it was true.

"And, I will," she said. "I need to talk to Darci, but then I'll call you."

The vehicle drew closer, tires crunching on the gravel.

"Can I kiss you?"

She nodded.

He leaned in, knowing he had only seconds before Garrison broke them apart.

It was a sweet kiss, an encouraging kiss. It wasn't anywhere near to the kiss he wanted from her, but it told him there was hope. She wasn't yet walking away.

The truck door slammed shut, and she drew back.

Riley stepped aside, watching as she turned and made her way to Garrison.

Once she was safely inside the truck, Garrison advanced on Riley.

Riley braced himself.

"That was gutsy," said Garrison, a note of what sounded like admiration in his tone as he came to a halt a few feet away.

The remark took Riley by surprise, and he didn't know how to answer.

Garrison's voice hardened. "Do it again, and I'll take your head off."

Riley knew how to answer that one. "Not necessary. Though I would like to see you try."

Garrison gave a brief glance to the truck, and his expression relaxed a fraction. "She didn't tell you to get lost?"

"She didn't."

Garrison nodded thoughtfully, and he turned back to Riley. "I've got my job to do. And I'm a professional. And I report to Shane Colborn." He paused. "But I gotta tell you. I think I'm pullin' for you."

With that, he walked away, leaving Riley momentarily stunned.

Garrison climbed into the driver's seat, reversing and heading for the exit.

Riley's gaze followed Kalissa's profile through the window. He hoped she'd call soon. He didn't think he could stand to wait.

"We agreed not to talk about you," Kalissa told her sister. "Either of you." She glanced to Shane who was glowering in the corner of the great room's alcove.

It was hard not to be intimidated by the castle-like size of the mansion, not to mention the stone work and the hundreds of antiques.

"How exactly is that going to work?" asked Darci.

"I'm not sure," Kalissa admitted. "There are some bugs we have to work out."

Darci looked uncomfortable. It was clear she was choosing her words carefully. "You know he's got some kind of vendetta against Shane."

"I don't want to hurt or upset you," said Kalissa.

"This isn't about me."

"I'm upset," said Shane, striding closer.

"No, you're not," said Darci. "You're ticked off."

"Oh, yes, I'm ticked off. He's an opportunistic lowlife. He's taking advantage of your sister."

"I know what I'm getting into," said Kalissa.

"Do you?" asked Shane. "He's doing this because of me. I can't stand by and—"

"It's not up to you," said Darci.

"I'm talking about a date," said Kalissa. "A simple date."

"She's not going to give away corporate secrets," said Darci.

"I'm not worried about corporate secrets," said Shane. "I'm worried about Kalissa. How are you going to feel when he breaks her heart?"

"My eyes are wide open," said Kalissa.

Shane clamped his jaw.

"If you like him," Darci said to Kalissa. "Then, you like him. It's not up to us to decide."

"I didn't mean for this to happen." Kalissa felt compelled to explain to her sister. "But there's something about him."

She wasn't ready to walk away from Riley. She figured it was a fifty-fifty chance he was conning her. But she was on alert now. She wouldn't accept anything he said at face value.

"Garrison stays," said Shane.

"Well, that's going to put a damper on the evening," said Darci.

"I'm in absolutely no danger from Riley," said Kalissa.

"It's beyond Riley," said Shane. "You're my sister-in-law. Somebody might mistake you for Darci. Riley or no Riley, you're vulnerable."

Kalissa came to her feet. "Now you're just making things up. You and Darci don't have any protection."

There was a beat of silence.

"We do," said Darci. "It's discreet. But we have a security staff."

"Seriously?"

Darci nodded.

Kalissa sat back down. "Are you in any danger?"

"No more or less than anyone else with family wealth."

"Am *I* in danger?" Kalissa had never thought through the implications of being a carbon copy of Darci.

"It's nothing we can't handle," said Shane. "And it's definitely nothing specific. If there's ever anything specific, we'll tell you up front."

Kalissa struggled to wrap her head around the situation. She couldn't.

She swallowed. "Is Garrison going to be my BFF?"

Darci cracked a smile.

"Is there a problem with Garrison?" asked Shane. "We can assign someone else to you."

Kalissa waved away the suggestion. "Garrison is fine. I kind of like him. He argues with Megan a lot, but it's rather entertaining."

"When are you going out with Riley?" Darci asked.

A warm feeling pulsed through Kalissa when she thought

about having another date. She couldn't help a soft smile. "I'm guessing as soon as I call him."

Darci and Shane exchanged a look.

"See what I mean," said Shane, conviction in his tone.

Kalissa looked to Darci in confusion.

"He thinks you've fallen head over heels and you're not thinking straight."

"I always think straight." And right now Kalissa's thoughts were moving straight to Riley. She couldn't wait to call him.

"Get him to come here," said Shane.

Kalissa couldn't believe she'd heard right. "That would be a colossally bad idea."

"You can't chaperone them, darling," said Darci.

"You should stay the night," said Shane. "Better yet, move in."

Kalissa couldn't help but laugh.

"Or we can get you a suite in the building in town. It's centrally located, and security is great."

"You'd *get* me a suite?" Kalissa couldn't believe she'd heard him right.

"Yes. In the same building we're in."

"On the waterfront? In downtown Chicago?" The real estate values there were astronomical.

"You could visit Darci anytime you wanted, without even going outside in the winter."

"I can't get used to this," Kalissa said to Darci.

"It is a bit disorienting," Darci agreed. "We'd let you pay rent."

"You're on *his* side?"

"It's a nice building. We'd get two bedrooms. Megan could stay there with you."

Kalissa stood again, pacing toward the corner fireplace. "This is so wrong."

"It's an apartment," said Darci. "Sure, maybe a bit bigger and a bit better location than most. But it's still just a rental apartment."

"No way," said Kalissa.

"I'm going to browse around," said Darci.

"Good idea, sweetheart."

"You two are ganging up on me?" There was no way Kalissa could go along with this.

Darci gave a shrug. "What can I say? I'm sleeping with him. He'll always be on my side."

"*You're* the one on *his* side."

"Same difference."

"No, it's not."

"If it makes you feel any better," said Darci. "I want you to be my neighbor just as much as Shane does."

"It's a bad idea to rent from family." Kalissa was sure she'd read that somewhere.

"What could go wrong?" asked Darci. "No matter what happens, you'll still be my sister."

"We'll do it through a management company," said Shane. "You'll never even know Colborn owns the place."

Kalissa braced herself on the brick fireplace hearth. "What part of *no* are you not hearing?"

Darci looked at Shane. "No? Did she say no? I'm not sure I'm familiar with that concept."

Shane looked amused. "People don't say no to us, Kalissa."

"That's because you're filthy rich and can fire everybody around you."

"Sure. That and we donate to a lot of charities."

"I am *not* a charity."

"And this isn't a donation. It's the purchase of a capital asset, which you will rent from us."

"We're paying three-hundred and fifty dollars a month for the suite above the store."

"Deal," said Shane, and he held out his hand, walking toward her.

"Nice try."

"Deal, Kalissa," he repeated. "I'm going to do whatever it takes to make your sister happy."

Kalissa clasped her own hands firmly behind her back, refusing to shake on it. "In this instance, I am not helping you out one bit."

Nine

Riley couldn't help but smile at Kalissa's curiosity as she gazed out the window of his car at the darkening city.

"It would be easier," she said. "If I could just tell Garrison where we're going."

"Why should I make things easy for Garrison?"

Riley had nothing against Garrison. He really did seem like a decent guy. But who wanted a bodyguard on a date?

She glanced in the passenger side rear view mirror. "He's stuck at the last traffic light."

"I'm sure he's got a tracking device on you."

"What?" Kalissa glanced down at herself. "Really? Where?"

"Probably your phone."

"This is weird," she said.

"No kidding. It's a whole different world when you have their kind of wealth."

"It sounds like you're no slouch either, Mr. Ellis Aviation." There was an accusation in her tone.

"I'm slowly getting there."

"Not as slowly as me. So, where are we going, money-bags? Some swanky, five-star restaurant? Maybe a champagne harbor cruise?"

"We're heading away from the lake."

"So, not a cruise." She peered out the windows on all sides. "Not a lot of restaurants around here either. By the way, I can't believe you took me out for a pretzel dog on our first date."

"You liked the pretzel dog."

"Sure, but you could have done something a bit more impressive."

"It wasn't impressive?"

"Not really."

"Then I don't think you're going to be too impressed to-night either."

She straightened in her seat. "Well, this doesn't sound promising for you."

"Problem is, you come across as being so down to earth."

She cocked her head. "That's a problem?"

"I don't want to spoil you."

"How incredibly considerate."

"We can't have you turning into a princess."

"I don't know about that. Maybe I'd be a good princess."

"Then let your brother-in-law buy you a penthouse."

"You have to pretend you don't know about that. I shouldn't have said anything. I promised you and I wouldn't talk about them." Her voice was pure worry.

"But he seemed okay that we're going out?"

"Not particularly. But I'm an adult, and he can't exactly hold me prisoner."

Riley glanced in his mirror, seeing Garrison's headlights coming up fast. "He's giving it an awfully good shot."

"He claims it's safety, that him and Darci also—" Kalissa clamped her mouth shut.

"I don't think it's a state secret that the Colborns have security," said Riley.

"It's safer if I don't talk about them at all."

"That's a bit impractical. Are you going to talk to them about me?"

"Depends."

"On what?"

She gave him a saucy smile. "On what you do."

"You mean on what *we* do. Do women share that kind of thing with their sisters?"

"I don't know. Maybe. Probably. I've never been a sister before."

"Then I'll be sure to give you something to talk about."

He steered the car into a huge, arena parking lot.

"What is this?"

Then she obviously spotted the sign. "The Fall Home and Garden Show?"

He grinned. "I thought you might like to check out the competition."

A smile grew on her face. "This could be fun."

"And only fifteen bucks apiece to get in."

She feigned shock. "You're spending a whole thirty dollars?"

"I might even spring for some pizza."

"Be still my beating heart."

"And an ice-cream bar," he added, finding an empty spot three rows from the entrance.

They left the car and crossed to the main door. There, Riley purchased their tickets, and Kalissa went first through the turnstile.

"Dude," hissed a voice from behind him. It was Garrison, gesturing to the pop-up banners. "Are you *sure* about this?"

"Completely," said Riley.

"Do you need me to float you a loan?"

"No, I don't need a loan. She's going to love it."

"Have you *seen* her sister's house?"

"Once," said Riley, hating the memory he recalled. "But I don't think Kalissa is like that."

"They're *all* like that."

"I'm taking my chances." Riley moved through the turnstile.

He shook off the memory of his teenage trip to the mansion, and Dalton's disdainful face. Instead, he focused on Kalissa, coming up behind her and putting his hand on the small of her back.

"What first?" he asked.

"The outdoors section," she said. "I'm thinking we should put a pond in your yard."

"I'd go for a gas fire pit." He wasn't crazy about ponds.

"You don't want a waterfall, maybe some ceramic frogs?" She started walking along the wide, crowded aisle.

"I liked that gazebo thing in Oak Park."

She slowed to look at a rock pond display.

"I'm not putting in a pond," he stated.

"But it's adorable," she sing-songed. "Look at the birds, and the little train."

"Maybe if I was seven."

"I thought you wanted kids someday."

"That means I have to buy a train?"

"No. But you should put in a pond."

"Look at this?" he tightened the arm around her waist and propelled her to the fireplace display on the opposite side of the aisle. "Toasty warm, and all that comfy furniture."

"I do like the stonework," she said.

"Could you put a cover over it?" he asked, serious about the question. "Maybe set it up next to the spa?"

She considered the display piece. "With some kind of a chimney, sure."

"I'm thinking of cool, rainy nights. A naked dip in the hot tub, then wrapping up in cozy, white robes, a mug of hot chocolate laced with brandy while we snuggle on a cushy, outdoor sofa."

"Forget about the train," she said, her voice breathless. "You're getting a fireplace."

He tightened his hold and gave her a kiss on the temple. "Who cares about the kids."

"They'd love a waterfall and a pool."

"For that, I'd need a bigger yard."

"It's your fantasy. Fantasize a bigger yard."

"I'm serious."

"About what?"

"The fire pit."

She pulled away to look up at him. "Really?"

"Would you like it?"

"Sure. Who wouldn't? But they're pretty expensive."

He glanced at the nearby displays. "There are more over there. Tell me what you like. What would suit my yard?"

"Okay." She nodded, her expression growing serious as she walked toward the other backyard mock-ups.

He paused to take in the view from behind, her long legs and those cute, spike heeled sandals, the way her bright blue skirt flowed over her hips, the little geometric cut-outs near her shoulder blades, and the smooth, tanned length of her arms.

His gaze settled on her profile, and the way her shiny hair curled around her cheeks and the nape of her neck. She was a cut above everyone else in the room.

And then it hit him dead center of his brain. Garrison was right. Riley had screwed up.

This was definitely not the way a woman dressed to wander the home and garden show.

He caught up to her and put an arm around her shoulders. "Let's get out of here."

She looked up. "Huh?"

"Let's go."

"But I like this one." She pointed to a fireplace.

"This isn't much of a date."

"It's a fine date."

Fine? Yeah, that's what he was going for. *Fine.*

She pointed. "Look at those colors in the ashlar stone."

He didn't bother. "Let's go find some dinner."

"We should at least pick up a brochure."

He pulled out his phone and snapped the barcode. "Got it. I know a great place."

"Last time you said that, we ended up in a hotel room."

"No hotel. Just a restaurant."

Her forehead furrowed.

"Unless, that is, you want a hotel. Then I'm all in. We can do room service if you'd like."

She looked around the cavernous show. "We've barely seen anything here. What changed your mind?"

"You."

"How did I do that?"

"You're not dressed for a trade show."

"Well, I didn't expect to be going to a trade show."

"What did you expect?"

"I don't know."

He took her hand in his, holding it between them, moving up close and lowering his voice. "You picked that particular dress to wear tonight. What did you expect, Kalissa?"

Her eyes were luminous as she gazed up at him. "Honestly, that I wouldn't have it on for long."

Riley's brain flat-lined. Then it restarted, and the breath whooshed into his lungs. He moved for the exit, pulling her with him.

"Hello?" She quickly sorted her feet out beneath her.

"When I'm not meeting your expectations," he said. "You should speak up."

She laughed. "The trade show was fun."

"This date is obviously not reaching its potential."

"Are we going for dinner now?" she asked with mock innocence.

"Yeah, right." They breezed through the exit.

"What about Garrison?"

"Garrison can take care of himself."

"I mean, what's he going to think?"

"He'll think we're leaving."

"Where are we going?" she asked.

"My place. I will feed you. Eventually. But you can't toss something like that out on the table and not expect me to react."

"I expected you to react."

"Good."

"I'm not naïve, Riley."

"Good again." Every minute he was with her, he liked her better and better.

The wind was rushing through the parking lot. The smell of rain was in the air, and thunder rumbled in the distance as they quickly made their way to the car. He opened the passenger door.

She paused and placed the palm of her hand against his chest. "I really did like the trade show."

He covered her hand as the first fat raindrops hit the windshield. "You're going to like my place a lot better."

She smiled. "I like confidence in a man."

"Good. Get in."

She sat down, and he pushed the door shut, all but trotting around to the driver's side.

Lightning flashed in the distance, thunder catching up as he started the engine.

The rain opened up on top of them.

"Nice timing," she said.

He checked out the flashes above them and put the wipers on high. "We're driving straight into it."

"Better than running straight into it. Boy, did I pick the wrong shoes."

He stopped to look down at her feet. "I'll carry you. I love those shoes."

She wiggled her foot back and forth. "Bit of a change from the work boots."

"Bit of a change," he agreed, putting the car into reverse, telling himself he could wait the twenty minutes it took to get home. But then he was definitely peeling those shoes from her feet.

A puddle was already forming at the exit to the arena parking lot. He splashed through it, and took a left onto the four lane road, heading for the lineup of traffic lights, hoping for as many greens as possible.

"I was daydreaming about a spa day," she said. "A new pedicure, maybe a facial."

The first light was green, and he silently celebrated. "Why not do it?"

"It's expensive. But someday…"

"Someday when your company hits it big."

"Exactly."

He wanted to tell her he'd pay for a spa day. He'd happily pay for a dozen of them to make her smile like that. But Shane was busy trying to throw material things her way, and Riley didn't want to be like Shane.

The second light was green, and there was little traffic. He knew if he kept to the speed limit, the lights were fairly well synchronized along this stretch.

"It'll happen for you," he told her.

"We had to hire three more casual guys. Word of mouth seems to be making a difference for us."

"You do very nice work."

An air horn blasted through the dark.

Riley instantly spotted the bright headlights bearing down on Kalisssa's side of the car. Then he saw the skid of the on-coming truck's tires as they hydroplaned over the water, jack-knifing the trailer under the red light and into the intersection. It was headed right for them.

He slammed on his brakes and cranked the steering wheel. "Hang on!"

He turned them on a dime. The huge truck grill took out the driver's door mirror, and the car bounced against the angle of the trailer. It barely registered that they hadn't been crushed, when Riley's back tire hit a curb, flipping the car onto its roof, spinning them twice around on the median.

The first things that registered in Kalissa's mind were the strange voices above her head. For a second, she thought it was a television, then she wondered why there was a party going on in her bedroom.

She tried to open her eyes, but the light was too bright.

"Kalissa?" It was Darci's voice. "Honey, can you hear me?"

"Darci?" Kalissa's throat was parched and sore, and her voice came out as a croak.

"It's me."

Kalissa felt a cool hand smooth across her forehead. "What are you doing here?"

Could she be having a dream?

"There was an accident," said Darci. "You're in a hospital."

Kalissa opened, her eyes, recoiling and blinking rapidly against the bright light. She quickly turned her face to the side.

There were half a dozen people beside her bed, more beyond the glass windows of the room. Most wore hospital uniforms, many were moving around. Machines beeped and carts rolled along the corridor.

"How—" And then she spotted Riley in the small crowd. He had bandages on his hand and forehead, and his shirt was torn.

It all came back to her, the bright lights, the loud horn. She'd thought for sure she was about to die.

"Riley?" she managed.

"He's here," said Darci. "He only has scrapes and bruises."

"He could have killed her," came Shane's distinct voice.

Kalissa shook her head. "He saved me. The truck, it was—" She stopped talking to swallow. Why did her throat hurt so bad?

"You got hit on the head," said Darci. "But they took x-rays, nothing is broken."

"My throat hurts."

A nurse appeared. "Would you like some water?"

Kalissa nodded.

The nurse quickly produced a plastic glass with a straw.

"Can I sit up?" Kalissa's body ached, but nothing was acutely painful. She felt a little silly lying here while everyone stood around her.

The nurse nodded, and Shane pressed the button at the foot of the bed, cranking her up.

She took a sip of the water. It was cool and soothing.

"I don't understand why my throat hurts."

"You screamed," said Riley from a few feet away. "Pretty long and loud when we flipped over."

"Haven't you done enough?" Shane demanded.

"We flipped over?" Kalissa asked Riley, struggling to remember.

He moved forward, giving Shane a glare on the way past. "How much do you remember?"

"The big truck. The lights. The horn." She stopped to take a shuddering breath. "It was coming straight for me."

"His tires were hydroplaning," said Riley. "The driver couldn't stop for the light. He's pretty shaken up."

"Does he know we're okay?"

"He does."

"If you hadn't turned so fast." Kalissa tried to keep the tremor from her voice.

Riley took her hand. "I turned," he said.

She nodded. There wasn't a doubt in her mind that he'd saved her life.

"You're coming home with us," said Shane.

"No." She didn't want to go home with Darci and Shane. She still wanted to go home with Riley.

"It's not a choice," said Shane.

"I'm—"

Riley gently squeezed her hand. "Let them take care of you."

"I don't need to be taken care of. I'm fine. Nothing's broken."

"You're not fine. Not yet."

"I am."

"Try to move something, anything."

She frowned at him. But then she braced her hand on the rail and shifted on the bed. Pain shot through her lower back, radiating down her arms and legs and up her neck.

"Ouch," she admitted.

Darci patted her knee. "Just for a day or two. Let us pamper you."

"Megan needs me."

"Not like this, she doesn't," said Shane.

Kalissa looked up at Riley. She might be in pain, but she still wanted to be with him.

The look in his eyes told her he understood. He leaned down to whisper in her ear. "I'm not going anywhere. You heal. I'll be waiting."

She wanted to wrap her arms around his neck and hold him close, but it was too painful to move.

"You about done, Ellis?" asked Shane, voice hard.

Riley straightened. "Not nearly. But she needs her rest. Take her home."

The two men glared at each other.

She wanted to tell them to stop, to please stop, but she didn't have the energy.

Then Riley's expression became gentle. He leaned down and gave her a kiss. "Call me when you feel like it."

"I already feel like it."

He smiled at her. "Sleep first, eat something, maybe take a long bath. I'm sending you a gift card for a spa."

She opened her mouth to protest, but he put his finger across her lips.

"Don't bother," he said. And then he was gone.

Darci and a nurse helped her into her clothes. She felt even more silly riding in a wheelchair. Then again, she really didn't feel like walking all the way to the parking lot.

Garrison was in the hallway standing next to Shane, and he gave her an encouraging smile as they wheeled her out.

"Next time," Shane told Garrison in an undertone. "She rides with you."

"I'll try," said Garrison. "But, for what it's worth, the guy's got skills. He knows what he's doing."

"You said he was reckless."

"I said he was fast. I don't know how he avoided the semi. I thought she was dead."

Shane swore.

"That's enough," said Darci. "We're not going to keep re-hashing it. Kalissa is fine."

"I'm fine," Kalissa said from the wheelchair.

Or she would be fine. She'd be fine after something to eat and a good night's sleep.

The elevator doors slid open, and Shane took over from the nurse, pushing her over the sill.

"Do you think we could stop for a burger?" she asked. "Benny's on Ponderosa has a drive through."

"We're not going anywhere near Ponderosa," said Shane.

"We can go past Ponderosa," said Darci.

"We're going downtown," said Shane. "There's a deli, a pizza place, or steak and seafood all on the same block as the penthouse."

"I'll take anything on rye," said Kalissa, "with Dijon and tomatoes. Maybe some fries."

"That sounds pretty heavy," said Darci. "Would you rather have soup?"

"I hit my head, not my stomach. And I'm starving."

"We'll get you anything you want," said Shane. For the first time since Kalissa had woken up, his voice was sympathetic.

They descended to the admitting area, waiting while Garrison retrieved an SUV. She and Darci took the back seat, while Shane sat up front. Garrison drove.

She dozed off in the car, and it seemed like only seconds later that Shane was helping her to the penthouse.

Garrison did the sandwich run, and Darci lent her a pair of pajamas. Soon she was tucked in their penthouse guest bedroom in a comfy, king sized, four poster bed.

Darci arrived in the dim room with bags of sandwiches.

"Does Megan know what happened?" Kalissa asked.

Her purse and phone were on the other side of the room, and she really didn't feel like getting up again.

"Riley called her from the hospital."

"That was nice of him."

"You smile when you say that." Darci took a seat at the foot of the bed, leaning back against one of the posts.

"Did I?"

"You smiled when you saw him at the hospital too."

"I like him," said Kalissa.

Darci dug into the bags, extracting a wrapped sandwich. She leaned forward to hand it to Kalissa.

"Thank you," said Kalissa. "I'm really hungry."

Darci opened a second bag, this one brown instead of white. And Kalissa noticed two different logos on the outsides.

"He went to two places?" she asked.

"They don't have fries at the deli."

Kalissa was embarrassed. "He didn't have to hunt down fries for me."

"You wanted fries, Garrison got you fries."

"I can see I'm going to have to be careful what I ask for around here."

"You had a bad night. It's the least we could do."

"No," Kalissa disagreed, even as she accepted a carton of fries. "This is the *most* you could do. You're treating me like a princess."

"You are a princess."

Kalissa smiled, remembering Riley's comment.

"What?" asked Darci.

"Something Riley said."

Darci waited.

"He said he didn't want me to turn into a princess."

Darci munched down a fry. "Is he worried about that?"

"I told him you wanted to get me an apartment. I'm sorry. I know I promised I wouldn't talk to him about you. But that seemed innocuous. And I was rattled by the offer."

"You can talk to him about us," said Darci. "It seems overly complicated not to."

"I don't want to give anything away."

Darci's expression was serious. "Do you trust him?"

"I don't know. I like him. I'm attracted to him. I want to trust him. But I really don't know him."

Darci nodded. "It could still be a con. He's got a lot of motivation to get into your good graces." She took a bite of her sandwich.

"It doesn't seem like a con. At least, not when I'm with him. I was going to sleep with him again tonight."

Darci appeared at ease with the revelation. "You're over twenty-one."

Kalissa bit down on the stack of ham and turkey. It was tasty and supremely satisfying.

"What are you going to do now?" asked Darci.

"Eat then sleep."

"We should invite him over here."

"Him?"

"Riley."

Kalissa didn't think she could be hearing right. "We?"

"Shane and me. And you, of course."

Kalissa shook her head. "Bad idea. Very bad idea. I didn't take you for an idealist."

"I'm not," said Darci. "But it's pretty obvious there's something building between the two of you, and—"

"And it might die a quick death. Maybe my memory of the sex is skewed. He might not be that good."

"Did you drink a lot that night?"

"Some wine, nothing out of the ordinary."

"Then he was probably that good."

"I was about to find out." Kalissa grinned self-consciously. "If not for that stupid semi."

Fear came over Darci's expression. "When Garrison called, I was so scared. I thought I'd found you only to lose you."

Kalissa's heart contracted. She leaned forward and reached for her sister.

Darci's hand met hers halfway, and they held tight.

"You're not going to lose me," Kalissa promised.

"And you're not going to lose me. Not over Riley or Colborn Aerospace or anything else. Shane will come around."

"You *are* an idealist."

"Maybe." Darci's eyes twinkled with mischief as she smiled. "But I can pretty much get Shane to do whatever I want."

Ten

"I nearly killed her," Riley said to Ashton.

"The truck driver nearly killed her," Ashton responded. "You got her out of the way."

It was after five, but the afternoon shift was humming outside Riley's office at Ellis Aviation. They'd just won another European contract, and Riley was in talks with a Canadian airline for ten E-22s. The prospect of the Canadian contract should have been a relief. But it would only exacerbate the problem with the engine mounting bracket shortage.

"I'm not going to stay away from her," he told Ashton.

"Who's saying you should?"

The door suddenly opened, startling them both.

Shane stood there, his shoulders stiff, jaw clenched.

Riley came to his feet.

Shane spared a fleeting glance at Ashton.

"I wanted to tell you man to man," said Shane.

"I've said everything I'm going to say to you about Kalissa. Do your worst." Riley narrowed his gaze. "And then I'll do mine."

Shane took three paces into the room. "This isn't about Kalissa."

The statement took Riley by surprise.

Shane kept talking. "It's about the engine mounting brackets."

Riley narrowed in on Shane's expression. "What about them?"

"You were right."

"I know." Riley hadn't guessed about Shane's involvement, he knew it for certain.

"One of my department heads," said Shane. "He thought he was helping."

"He was helping. Helping you, at least."

Shane shook his head. "It wasn't on my orders."

Riley didn't believe it for a second. "Are you here to throw him under the bus?"

"I had no idea."

"You got caught, Shane. Own up to it."

"Are you calling me a liar?"

"Yes."

Shane's complexion turned ruddy.

Ashton stood.

Shane looked Ashton up and down. "I don't want any trouble."

"You look like you do," said Ashton.

"It's fine," said Riley. He wasn't afraid of Shane.

"I fired him for it," said Shane. "But you go ahead and believe whatever you want."

"I generally do."

"I don't do business that way. I don't have to."

Riley hated to admit it, but Shane's words had a ring of sincerity to them. Shane might resent the hell out of Riley but, aside from that ludicrous tell-all book by the ex-girlfriend, Riley had never heard talk of Shane being dishonest.

Then again, there was one way to find out for sure.

"Then I guess you'd be willing to walk it back?" Riley asked. "Sell them to me at wholesale?"

It was clear Shane hadn't anticipated the request. "You haven't found another source?" Then he gave a harsh laugh. "You obviously haven't found another source, or else you'd force me to keep my capital tied up."

"I found another source," said Riley. "But at a higher cost."

"So you're suggesting we help each other?"

"I'm suggesting we don't harm each other."

"That'll be novel," said Shane.

"Won't it just?"

They both stood their ground, until Shane gave a sharp nod.

Riley's opinion of him went up the smallest of notches. "You actually fired him?"

Shane's nod was grim. "There are lines you don't cross."

Riley tried to square Shane's apparent moral framework with a man who continued to shun him as a half-brother. He couldn't.

Shane stared out the office window to the plant floor. "It's bigger than I expected."

"We're growing," said Riley.

"Tetralast robotics?" asked Shane.

"Maybe."

Shane turned and gave him a knowing smirk. "We've got them too."

"You going to give me a tour of Colborn?"

"Nope."

"Then stop checking out my shop."

Shane put his back to the window. "You can talk to David Gorman about the engine mounting brackets."

"And Kalissa?" asked Riley, hoping this might be an opportunity to clear the air.

"She says she's going home tomorrow."

"I know."

"Garrison's staying with her."

"I know that too. For the record, I don't disagree."

"That's *such* a relief," Shane drawled.

Riley considered his brother. "I think it's our destiny to duke it out. And I wouldn't care about that, except neither of us can stay away from Kalissa."

"You can stay away from her."

"No." Riley shook his head. "I can't."

Shane seemed to think for a minute. "We could ignore each other," he offered.

The suggestion struck Riley as elegantly ironic. "I guess it's worked well enough for the last thirty years."

Shane's gaze narrowed in what looked like puzzlement but had to be irritation. He was obviously intent on keeping up the façade through thick and thin.

Fine with Riley. Right now, he was only interested in Kalissa.

* * *

A hurricane lamp flickered in the center of the hewn, polished table, and the perimeter lighting glowed orange against rustic walls of the steakhouse. Kalissa's big, leather chair was soft and comfortable, the music was pleasant and the conversation from the other diners was muted in the distance.

"I'm not trying to be clever this time," said Riley from across the table. "I'm not trying to be richer or poorer than I really am."

"Were you trying to be clever before?" she asked.

"I thought the garden show was clever. And I thought the pier would prove to you that I was a regular guy."

"And when you slapped down your credit card for a one-use, designer dress?"

"I was trying to impress you."

"And now?"

"Now." He reached across the table and took her hands in his. He had sexy hands, square, strong, smooth to the touch.

"Now I only want you to be comfortable."

"I am comfortable. These chairs are great."

"You're not sore?"

"I'm back to normal." She was at the job site most of the day with Megan, and she still felt fine. "I suppose I'm a little spoiled from staying at the penthouse. There's a chance I've turned into a princess."

He gave her hands a squeeze. "Whatever will we do about that?"

"My single bed and the bare light bulb above the Mosaic shop should cure me."

"Is that where you're planning to sleep?"

"Did you think I'd go back to Darci's?" She was surprised that he'd assume that about her.

"No." He drew out the word, putting a wealth of meaning into his tone as he smoothed the pad of his finger across her knuckles.

"Ahhh, you have a third option."

"I have a third option."

Kalissa had a feeling she was going to like the third option.

"You two ought to be ashamed of yourselves!" The strident voice of a woman interrupted them.

Kalissa's glance shot up to see a rotund, neatly dressed, fifty something woman bearing down on their table.

"Excuse me?" she asked in surprise.

"Ma'am, this is a private dinner," said Riley.

"Shameless," said the woman, smacking their joined hands. "Utterly shameless."

Riley jumped to his feet. "I'm going to ask you politely to—"

"What do you think you're doing?" a male voice boomed.

This time it was a man, likely in his thirties. He was tall, burly, wearing an expensive suit with a silk tie encircling his thick neck. He grasped Riley's arm.

Riley wrenched away. "Back off."

"Don't touch my mother," boomed the man.

"Tell your mother this is a private dinner."

"I'm telling your husband," the woman barked at Kalissa.

"I don't have a husband," Kalissa responded.

Another large man joined the first, boxing Riley against the table.

A waiter rushed over. "Is there a problem here?"

"Shane Colborn is a good man," said the woman. "He donated to the animal shelter." She suddenly grabbed Kalissa's wine glass, tossing the merlot, splashing Kalissa in the chest.

Riley jerked forward, and the two men lunged, one of them hitting him square in the stomach.

"Riley," Kalissa yelled.

Next thing she knew, a strong arm was around her shoulders.

"Take her," Riley yelled above her head. "Get her out of here." He returned the man's punch, then he ducked as the second man aimed a shot at his head.

Kalissa struggled against the arm.

"It's me," Garrison rumbled in her ear. "Come on."

"No." She wasn't abandoning Riley.

"I need you safe."

"No!"

"Then I can help him."

Reality hit Kalissa, and she started to move willingly away from the table. "Go," she said to Garrison. "Go back."

He banged open a black, swinging door that led to the kitchen.

"Keep her in here," he ordered a man in a chef's uniform.

The man nodded, and Garrison disappeared back through the door.

Kalissa couldn't believe it. How could it be happening? This was a classy place. How could a misunderstanding degenerate into a fist fight?

Shouts came through the door. Glass broke and something thudded against a wall.

The chef was on the phone, talking to the police, asking for immediate assistance. Kalissa was terrified for Riley and Garrison. She was desperate to see what was going on, but she was afraid the sight of her would only make things worse.

Then the two of them all but exploded through the doorway. Sweaty and disheveled, they each grasped one of her arms.

"Nearest exit?" Riley shouted to the chef.

"Fire exit." He pointed with his thumb. "But you'll set off the alarm."

"Okay by me," said Garrison, and the two of them pulled Kalissa along, her feet barely touching the floor.

"Are you guys okay?" she asked breathlessly as they wound their way around counters, grills and produce bins.

The entire staff had stopped working and gaped at them as they passed.

"We're fine," said Riley. "Keep going."

"Here," said Garrison, pointing to a door.

Riley pushed on the crash bar and shoved it open. An alarm sounded, and a light flashed above.

They rushed down a flight of wooden stairs, ending up in an alleyway.

"My car's right there," said Garrison.

"You parked in the alley?" Kalissa asked.

"I always park in the alley. It makes for a quick exit."

"This has happened before?" She had a hard time wrapping her head around that.

"Mostly with rock stars," said Garrison.

He opened a back door, and Riley pushed Kalissa inside. He followed her.

Garrison jumped in up front.

Riley turned to her, while Garrison started the engine.

"Are you hurt?" he asked.

"I'm fine. But I don't think my dress survived." The pale blue fabric was stained with red wine.

Riley cracked a smile, while Garrison glanced in the rear view mirror, a sparkle in his eyes.

"That woman was nasty," said Kalissa. "Not to mention judgmental."

Then both men coughed out a laugh.

"It wasn't funny," said Kalissa. "That was embarrassing."

"You didn't do anything to be embarrassed about," said Riley.

"Do we need to talk to the police?" she asked.

It felt as if they were fleeing the scene of a crime.

"I'll take care of it," said Garrison. "I know a bunch of guys at the precinct."

"Thanks for your help in there," said Riley.

"Thanks for yours," Garrison returned. "It caught me off guard. I wasn't expecting trouble in a place like that." He paused. "Lesson learned."

"I should have worn black," said Kalissa. "Lesson learned."

"The dress is replaceable," said Riley.

"What am I supposed to do, stay locked inside my house?" It wasn't like she could stop looking like Darci.

"I'm going to recommend you two do an interview," said Garrison. "Something on network television. We'll get the story out there, with your picture together, so people know there's two of you. That way this kind of thing will stop happening." He changed lanes and then retrieved his cell phone.

Riley leaned in and squeezed Kalissa's hand. "Are you sure you're okay?"

"I'm peachy. Hungry, but peachy. Any chance we're going by a drive-through?"

"We are *not* getting fast food tonight."

Garrison spoke into his phone. "There was a disturbance at the restaurant."

"You'd rather I starve?" asked Kalissa.

"She's fine," said Garrison. "She's with me. We're in the car."

"We'll go someplace else," said Riley. "Someplace quiet and discreet."

"That place was quiet and discreet."

"Got it," said Garrison, and he ended the call. He pocketed his phone. "Shane wants me to bring her to the penthouse."

"No," said Riley with a definitive shake of his head. "Our last date ended with her at Shane's penthouse. It's not happening again."

"Maybe I should just go home," said Kalissa, trying not to sound self-pitying.

"Take us to the Emerald Hotel," said Riley. "It has a secure floor, and we can order room service."

Garrison answered with a nod. Then he gave a wry smile. "Well, that'll be a fun conversation for me to have with Shane."

"Tell him I insisted," said Riley.

"Tell him *I* insisted," said Kalissa. She'd only seen the Emerald Hotel from the outside, but it was stately and elegant. She had high hopes for the room service menu.

Maybe they could salvage this date after all.

Riley checked in while Garrison waited.

Kalissa had taken a seat in the corner of the lobby. She was hunched over, clearly self-conscious about her stained dress. It was probably just as well she was keeping a low profile, Riley decided. She looked like an extra from a low budget horror flick—an adorable extra, for sure. But at first glance, somebody might dial 911.

"She's not going home tomorrow," Riley said to Garrison as they walked away from the counter.

"She's never going home," said Garrison.

Riley agreed on that. Making her relationship to Darci public would solve one set of problems, but it would create another. The sister-in-law of a prominent city billionaire couldn't live above a landscaping shop in a sketchy part of town.

"Tell Shane to arrange whatever it takes," said Riley. "I won't fight him on it."

"I doubt I'll have to tell Shane anything."

"True enough," said Riley as they left the check-in counter. This was one instance where Shane's take-charge attitude was a plus. "Can you let Megan know she won't be home tonight?"

"Will do."

Kalissa saw them approaching and came to her feet.

"I'll call you in the morning," Riley said to Garrison.

"Stay put until we talk."

"No problem." Riley would happily keep Kalissa safe and cloistered inside a hotel room for as long as it took.

Garrison peeled off with a wave, and Riley took her hand. "Elevator's this way."

"My life is completely out of control," she said as she fell into step with him.

"For tonight, it's completely under control."

"I'm in a five star hotel, in a stained dress, with no luggage and a vigilante grandmother after me."

A uniformed attendant checked the key card before allowing Riley to swipe it and open the secure floor elevator.

"Is he armed?" Kalissa whispered, glancing back as they walked through the doorway into the cherry paneled, gilded mirror elevator.

"I have no idea."

There was a single button on the panel for the thirty-second floor.

"Even if he's not," she said. "I bet he can keep the rogue grandmothers out."

"I'm betting he can too. You're not nervous are you?"

"I'm annoyed, and I'm sticky, but I'm not nervous."

He took in the big stain. "We really are going to have to replace that dress."

"Do you suppose the room will have bathrobes?"

"I'm sure it will."

The elevator came to a stop, the doors gliding open.

"Because I'd really love to take a shower and change."

"Go for it."

The suite was a very short walk, and Riley swiped the key.

The door opened to a big, bright living room with peach and gold sofas, an oak dining table for six, and a gas fireplace with a pale, fieldstone hearth. There were paintings on the walls and decorator touches in the lamps and knickknacks. A set of double doors at the far end led to the bedroom.

Kalissa stopped in the foyer and stared around the place. "Why didn't you just get a regular room?"

He latched the door behind them. "There are no regular rooms on this floor."

"This is enormous."

"I doubt we'll get lost."

"How much—"

"Don't worry about it."

"But—"

"You're safe here. That's all that matters. And nobody is going to bother us." He shrugged out of his jacket and tossed it on the arm chair. Then he loosened his tie. "We're going to relax and enjoy the rest of the evening."

She looked down at her ruined dress. "I'm definitely getting out of this."

He pointed to the bedroom doors. "Try in there."

She drew a resigned sigh, then she gave him a brave smile and headed into the bedroom.

Riley eased down on the sofa, shaking out his skinned knuckles and checking his phone for messages.

"They have robes," she called from the depths of the bedroom. She sounded excited.

Riley chuckled to himself. In a place like this, he could probably have an entire wardrobe sent up for her. But she was going to look great in the simple white bathrobe.

He heard the water go on, and he couldn't help picturing her in the shower, water glistening on her skin, soap suds coursing over her breasts, down her stomach, lower...

He shook his head, telling himself to focus on something else. There were a few messages from work, and he opened one of them, hitting a link to a financial report.

"Riley?" she called.

"Yeah?"

"You've got to come and see—"

He was on his feet halfway across the room before she finished the sentence.

"—the shower heads in here. Oh, hi."

Her smile was bright, and she was completely naked, standing inside the oversize, tiled cubicle.

"They shoot out from everywhere." She pointed to the half dozen spray nozzles.

He stripped off his tie and started on the shirt buttons.

"You're coming in?" she asked sweetly, her eyes dancing with mischief as she backed under the spray.

"I hope you're not too hungry," he told her, tugging off his pants.

She gave a mock pout. "It's happening a lot lately. I'm getting used to it."

"Here's a tip." He stepped into the hot spray. "Don't get naked and wet." He slid his arms around her hot, dripping body. "And don't be so incredibly gorgeous if you want me to focus on food."

She grinned and wound her arms around his neck. "Who says I'm hungry for food?"

She was hot and slick and soft against him, all curves and sweet spots. He ran his hands from her shoulders, to her back, over the curve of her rear, down the tops of her thighs.

"I've missed you," she whispered.

He hugged her tight, cradling her head against his chest, desperate to absorb and memorize everything, her scent, her touch, her taste. He blocked the spray with his back, tipping her chin, kissing her deeply.

Her tongue tangled with his, while her hands slid down his body, kneading his thighs, moving between them while the water rushed along his skin.

"Oh, sweetheart," he groaned. "Don't—"

"Don't?" There was a smile in her voice, and her grip tightened. "Are you sure? Don't?"

He groaned, gritting his teeth against the avalanche of sensations. "You're playing with fire."

"So, burn me."

He drew back to look at her.

Her eyes were opaque, her pupils dilated. Her skin was flushed, her lips dark red and parted, and her hair was mussed in a damp halo around her face.

"Do it now," she whispered. "Right now."

He lifted her, stepping forward so that her back was braced against the tile wall, wrapping her legs around his hips. Waiting was no longer an option, and he entered her in one smooth stroke.

"Riley," she moaned, clinging to him as he moved. "Yes. Oh, so yes."

"You have no idea how much I've missed you."

He kissed her neck, tasting its sweetness with the hot water droplets. He braced her firmly, increasing his pace, desire singing through his bloodstream, pushing him forward, blocking out everything but Kalissa.

"Faster," she told him. "Harder. Just…Oh…"

He increased their pace, the water pounding on his back, her breath in his ear, her scent surrounding him.

And then she cried out, her entire body convulsing around him.

He followed her over the edge, clinging tight as wave after

wave of ecstasy nearly buckled his knees. The pulses gradually subsided, and he realized his grip on her was too tight.

He eased back. "Sorry."

"For *what*?"

"It felt like I was crushing you."

"I didn't notice."

He smiled into her face and smoothed back her wet hair. "You are amazing."

"You're no slouch yourself."

"That was fast."

Her grin widened. "That was great. And I figure we've got all night."

"You figure right." He gave her a kiss.

"Do you think a girl could get a steak around here? Or maybe some chicken or pasta?"

He backed up so they were both under the spray again. "I'd say this girl could get pretty much anything she wanted."

Kalissa sat next to Riley on the king sized bed. They were both wrapped in hotel robes, finishing their wine while she flipped through news channels on the flat screen.

"Who do you think would want to interview us?" she asked.

She understood Garrison's plan, but she wasn't sure there'd be that much public interest in her and Darci.

"Any of the talk shows in Chicago," said Riley.

"I don't much like talk shows."

"You don't have to like them to be on one."

She continued flipping channels, through a couple of sitcoms and some sports games. "I like garden shows."

"No surprise there."

"And the ones with people buying real estate. That looks like a lot of fun."

"You want to buy some real estate?"

"It's not in my immediate future. But the people always seem really happy on those shows. It's usually a couple, sometimes some kids. They're embarking on a new chapter of their lives. I don't know, there's an energy to it all."

"Maybe you and Darci should go real estate shopping together. You could bring along a camera crew."

"Oh, sure. They could show the pathetic, impoverished relative being rescued by her benevolent, wealthy sister."

"That's not what I meant."

She knew it wasn't. And she was trying not to be sensitive. But she valued her independence, and it felt like it was eroding away.

He reached over and touched the bottom of her chin, gently urging her to look at him. "Hey."

"I know it's not what you meant." She regretted her reaction.

"Darci doesn't want to upset you. Even Shane doesn't want to upset you."

It wasn't what they did, it was who they were that was messing with her life.

"I'll handle it," she said with determination. "I am handling it."

"I've no doubt you will," he said. Then his tone changed. "But you do understand that your life has changed."

She focused her gaze on her lap, rolling the robe's flat belt into a spiral. "It doesn't have to change that much."

"It already has."

She fought a growing panic in the pit of her stomach. "I don't care about their money. I don't want their money."

"I think they know you're not a gold-digger."

"I can take care of myself."

"Under normal circumstances, yes. But these are not normal circumstances."

She didn't answer. She wanted to argue that tonight was an anomaly. What were the chances she'd run into another rabid Shane Colborn fan who felt it their duty to protect his marriage?

But she still remembered the day at the discount store. It was going to happen again, probably not every day, and probably not so dramatically, but there were going to be mix-ups. And she might find herself in embarrassing or dangerous circumstances again.

Riley tucked her hair behind one ear, giving him a better view of her profile. "You have to let Shane protect you."

"You hate Shane."

"I don't hate Shane. I don't like him. Okay, maybe I hate him. But that doesn't make him wrong."

"He wants me to landscape his mansion."

"That doesn't surprise me."

She unrolled the belt and started over. "He wants that to be my full time job."

"If I had a mansion," said Riley. "I'd want you to landscape it too."

"Would you try to buy me an apartment?"

"I'd buy you anything you wanted."

"Then thank goodness you're not a billionaire. I'd be a spoiled princess in no time."

Riley was silent for a long time, and for some reason, the silence felt tense.

She let go of the belt and rolled up on her knees, facing him. "If you had a mansion, I'd definitely landscape it for you."

He gave what looked like a weak smile. "Glad to hear it."

She wiggled in, cupping his face in her hands. It was rough with stubble, and his hair had dried in a mess. His eyes were soft gray. She loved his eyes. She loved his mouth. It was so incredibly kissable.

"Again?" he asked in a tone of surprise.

"I was only going to kiss you."

"You're trying to distract me."

That wasn't true. She'd wanted to look at him, touch him, breathe him in. But she wasn't ready to admit how badly she was falling for him.

So, she smiled and pretended it was only about sex. "Is it working?"

He glanced meaningfully down at her gaping robe. "What do you think?"

"I think you turn me on." She kissed his mouth.

He pulled her into his lap. "I think we need to have this conversation."

"You want to talk about sex?"

"I want you to be safe."

"I am safe." She turned so that she was straddling him.

He took a long look at her body through the parted robe. But then he pulled the two lapels together and held them there. "I want you to go with Garrison tomorrow and then do whatever Shane tells you."

"And if he tells me to stay away from you?"

"Ignore that part."

"He'll move me into his building." It felt fundamentally wrong to let Shane and Darci do that.

"You know you can't stay where you are."

She put her hands over his, easing them from the robe until it fell open again. "I'm staying exactly where I am right now."

"You are shameless."

She leaned forward. "Can we talk about this tomorrow?"

His lips brushed hers. "Say yes."

"Yes."

"Yes, what?"

"Yes, I'll do what I'm told."

His hands moved to bracket her hips. "Do you know how incredibly sexy that sounds?"

"I'm half naked in your bed, and we've been apart for two weeks. Everything I say sounds incredibly sexy."

She kissed him, shifting so that their bodies pressed together.

He spoke softly against her lips. "You are also incredibly right."

Then he enfolded her in his arms, and she let reality slip away.

Eleven

Kalissa knew she had well and truly fallen through the looking glass. She stood next to Megan gaping at the two bedroom apartment.

"It's only a temporary rental," said Darci. "It would be nice, when we buy, to get something on a higher floor."

"I can see the lake clearly from here," said Megan, gesturing out one of the bay windows in the spacious living room.

The apartment was fully furnished, with a forest green sectional sofa, coordinating green and white striped armchairs, glass and brass tables dotting the living area, with a big, round glass topped table in the dining alcove. In the middle of it all, was a round, gas fireplace with beach rocks and a see-through chimney.

The kitchen was decked out with state of the art, stainless steel appliances, a massive island and pure, white countertops. The hallways led to two big bedrooms, each with its own en suite bathroom, and each of which led onto the wraparound deck.

"We have a right of first refusal on anything that comes up for sale in the building," said Darci. "There are two units expected to be listed next month."

"I know I keep saying this," said Kalissa. "But this is too much. It's too big. It's too opulent."

"It's what was available," said Darci.

"When you buy, can it be something smaller?"

Darci exchanged a glance with Garrison who was standing in the doorway. He was either guarding it or giving the three women a wide berth.

Megan obviously noticed their look. "I don't think they come any smaller," she said to Kalissa.

"I'm not going to be able to get used to this."

"Well, I am," said Megan. "Never mind a bedroom, we each get our own bathroom."

"Which one do you want?" Kalissa asked.

Megan laughed. "Yeah, I think you get the master."

"Not necessarily."

"I'm just along for the ride."

"So am I," said Kalissa.

Darci looked to Garrison again.

He stepped forward. "Megan, I think we should go get some of your things together."

His words seemed to take Megan by surprise. "My things?"

"From the old place. Yours and Kalissa's."

"I'll come help," said Kalissa.

"Stay here with me," said Darci.

"*You're* going to help me pack boxes?" Megan asked Garrison with obvious disbelief.

"They'll need me," said Kalissa.

"I'm going to help you talk to the movers," Garrison said to Megan. "They'll pack the boxes."

"Stay," Darci said to Kalissa. "We've got some things to discuss."

"But…" Kalissa couldn't let everyone else do her work.

"They're professional movers," said Darci. "They won't break anything."

"I'm not worried about breakage."

Garrison opened the door and gestured to Megan.

"I can take a hint," Megan breezily told him as she strode for the door.

"Are you thirsty?" asked Darci.

Kalissa watched the door close behind the pair, feeling like she'd missed something important.

"Thirsty?" she asked.

"There's a wine cooler in the pantry." Darci made her way to the kitchen.

"It has wine in it?" Kalissa asked.

It was early afternoon, but it was one of the strangest days of her life. Wine wouldn't be the worst thing in the world.

"Shane had them move some bottles from the cellar last night."

"These are from the mansion?"

"They are," said Darci, selecting a bottle.

"Not the good stuff."

Darci laughed. "Don't let Shane hear you say that. He'll tell you it's all the good stuff."

Kalissa supposed that was true.

She moved closer to Darci. "You have to slow down. It's making me horribly uncomfortable."

"We should chat," said Darci, pressing the button on an electric corkscrew. "There are glasses hanging above the island."

"How does this place have wine glasses?" Appliances, Kalissa could understand, even furniture and the odd painting. But dishes?

"Sometimes people only rent it for a weekend. It's nice if it has all the amenities."

Kalissa wanted to ask how much they were paying, but she was afraid of the answer. Instead, she retrieved two wine glasses.

Darci crossed to the table. "We'll let it breathe for a minute." She sat down at one end.

Kalissa took the chair next to Darci's. They were padded and upholstered, and ridiculously comfortable for dining chairs.

"I haven't told you much about our father," said Darci.

"That's okay." Kalissa knew that Ian Rivers had been unhappy with his life and not particularly successful.

"No, it's not okay. There are things you need to understand. The first one is that our dad was once very close to Dalton Colborn."

"Really?" The revelation surprised Kalissa. "I thought you only met Shane in the spring."

"I did. Dad and Dalton went to school together. They opened a company together. They invented a turbine together. But then it all fell apart."

"What happened?"

"They fought. Dalton stole the turbine designs, and for some reason our father never went after him. I think he tried at first but gave up."

"So our dad was an engineer?" That was impressive.

"A good one, it turns out. When he died, well, I told you I spied on Shane."

Kalissa nodded.

"I did it to prove Dalton was a criminal, and that Shane's fortune was based on the theft of our father's intellectual property."

Now Kalissa was intrigued. "And that's how you met Shane?"

"He caught me spying."

Kalissa couldn't help but smile. She knew enough about Shane's temper to guess it hadn't been pretty.

"But he fell for you anyway?"

Darci smirked. "I guess I'm irresistible." She lifted the bottle of wine. "But, here's the thing. I had the last laugh. I proved our dad had invented the turbine."

Kalissa sat back in amazement. She had no idea what to say.

Darci started to pour. "You know I own half of Colborn?"

Kalissa didn't know the details, but Shane had made a few jokes about Darci's ownership. "Okay."

"That's not because I married Shane. It's because I could have sued him and won."

"You were going to *sue* Shane?"

Darci set down the bottle. "Here's the thing and, by the way, this is a very fine bottle of wine."

Kalissa glanced reflexively at the label.

"Our dad, your birth father, should rightly have owned half of Colborn." Darci lifted one of the glasses.

Kalissa quickly picked up the other.

"Congratulations, Kalissa Smith. Twenty-five percent of Colborn Aerospace belongs to you."

Kalissa nearly dropped the glass.

She couldn't form a word. She couldn't ask a question. Her vocal cords had frozen completely stiff.

Darci grinned as she touched her glass to Kalissa's.

"*What*?" Kalissa finally managed to sputter.

Darci drank. "We're in this together, sister. Take a drink."

"What? No. *No*."

"Yes," said Darci. "Drink."

Kalissa sat with her jaw hanging open.

Darci pushed the glass toward her. "It's not official until you take a drink."

"It's not official at all."

"Ah, but it is."

Kalissa did take a swallow of her wine. A big one.

Darci set down her glass. "Okay, that was fun."

"Fun? You think that was *fun*?"

"I know it's a bit freaky right at first. But you'll get used to it."

Kalissa came to her feet. "I'll get *used* to being a billionaire? It's not like a new haircut."

"It is, in a way."

Kalissa blinked at her sister in complete stupefaction.

"Well, a radical haircut. You have to start thinking of yourself in a new way. I'm glad you like Garrison, because he's not going away. From now on you won't have to worry about money. You can pay off whatever business debts you have, and grow your business a lot faster than you'd planned. That's all good, right?"

Kalissa dropped back into the chair.

"I'd have another drink if I was you," said Darci.

Kalissa took her advice. "This is insane."

"Yeah." The teasing look went out of Darci's eyes, and she topped up their glasses. "But I've been through it myself, and I'm here to help."

"Could you wake me up?"

That would be the most helpful thing Darci could do at the moment.

"You don't have to do anything right away," said Darci. "Settle in here. There are some papers to sign."

Kalissa felt a ray of hope. "What if I don't sign them?"

Darci shrugged. "It won't help. Shane has very good lawyers. We'll get you one way or the other." Her gaze went soft, eyes almost teary. "Our father would be so thrilled, *so thrilled* by this. We're together. And he's been exonerated. I know it's a lot to take in. But it feels so right. I've never been happier."

Kalissa squeezed her eyes shut. "A billionaire."

"Technically, only a quarter billionaire. But I'm sure you'll find a way to scrape by. First off, there are the clothes. And you'll never have to fly coach again."

Kalissa was too overwhelmed to laugh at the joke. "Who else knows?"

"So far, just me, Shane and a couple of lawyers."

"Can we keep it a secret?"

"For as long as you want. Well, you know, within reason. You don't have to be scared of this, Kalissa."

"Really? Because right now I'm terrified."

"We also told Garrison. It's not a good idea to keep secrets from your security people."

Kalissa could live with that.

"I just want to be normal," she said. Then she did laugh. "All right, as normal as I can be right now. Just for a little while longer."

For some reason, she dreaded telling Riley. He might not care. It might not change things between them. But she wasn't ready to take that chance.

Riley wasn't going to let Shane keep him away from Kalissa. Ellis aviation had just won the Canadian contract, and Shane was going to be massively annoyed. But that wasn't stopping Riley from showing up at her door.

The security desk had his name and let him straight through. So he headed up in the elevator. He'd brought along a large pizza and a six pack of imported beer, guessing Megan would be around on a Sunday night.

It was Megan who opened the door, but there were other voices behind her.

"Hi, Riley." She greeted him with a smile, pulling the door open. "Come on in."

Garrison was also in the room, as were Shane and Darci. Perfect.

"It's Riley," Megan called out, relieving him of the pizza box.

"Yum," she said to him.

Kalissa gave him a smile and rose to her feet, crossing to meet him. Behind her back, Shane scowled. Riley assumed he'd either heard about the new contract or about him and Kalissa having spent the night together. Either way, they'd agreed to ignore each other, and that was exactly what Riley intended to do.

He gave Kalissa a hug and a quick kiss. "Settling in?" he asked her.

"Getting thoroughly spoiled. Did you know The Range Club delivers steak and crab?"

Riley couldn't help but glance at the simple pizza box Megan had set on the dining table. Maybe he should have added the morel mushrooms.

"Didn't know that," he said.

"They were amazing."

"So, you're off corndogs, then?"

She gave him an odd look, and he realized there'd been a defensive edge to his voice.

"Nice place," he said to change the subject.

She glanced around. "It seemed huge at first. But I'm getting used to it."

Riley couldn't help but think that had happened fast. He shot another quick glance in Shane's direction, encountering his hostile stare. Was that his plan? Make her want the good life, knowing that he could give her more than Riley?

"Come on," said Kalissa. "Sit down."

She kept hold of his arm, leading them to one of the sofas.

Directly in front of him were the fireplace and a bay window overlooking the lake. Closer still was Shane's glare.

"I'll give you the tour later," said Kalissa. "But the other rooms are full of boxes."

"That's why we didn't cook," said Megan. "Anybody want pizza?"

Nobody took her up on the offer. Riley was hungry, but he'd wait.

"We don't end up doing a lot of cooking," said Darci.

Unlike Shane, she didn't seem irked with Riley. He hoped that was a good sign.

"I had the best of intentions," she said. While she spoke, Shane took her hand. "But everything is so close and so convenient. It was easy to get lazy."

"You're not lazy," said Shane.

"Well, Kalissa and I are still on a budget," said Megan.

Darci and Kalissa seemed to exchange a look.

"Good thing Colborn has accounts at the nearby restaurants," Shane casually tossed out. "Just give them our name."

Riley couldn't help smirking at that offer. Shane was playing this well.

"We can't do that," said Megan.

She looked at Kalissa, who was gazing at Darci.

"Thanks, Shane," said Kalissa. "That's very nice of you."

Riley felt himself stiffen.

"Are you *kidding*?" asked Megan. "We have carte blanche at five star restaurant takeout?"

"Only if we start using the stairs to wear off the calories," Kalissa said with a laugh that sounded slightly strained.

"Do we need more wine?" Darci asked brightly, coming to her feet.

Shane stood. "I can—"

"No, darling. Kalissa? Can you give me a hand?"

"If you don't need me anymore tonight, Mr. Colborn," Garrison said, rising.

"We're fine," said Shane. "Thanks."

Garrison gave him a nod. Then he turned to Megan. "Do you want me to move that box before I go?"

Megan's brow went up. "Box? Oh, yes please, the box. I'd forgotten about it." She unfolded her legs and pulled herself out of the deep armchair.

Kalissa and Darci went to the kitchen, while Garrison and Megan headed down the hall.

"You think you can keep up the pace?" Shane asked.

"I can afford all the steak and crab she wants."

Shane looked momentarily confused. "I meant the Canadian jet deal."

Riley gave himself a mental shake. "You heard?"

"Of course, I heard. You're spreading yourself pretty thin."

Riley wasn't worried. Well, he wasn't too worried. Maxing out capacity wasn't without its risks. "Maybe I'll hire some of your staff."

"Maybe I'll back out of the Dubai, Britain and California bids. I left myself an out clause. I'm betting you didn't. If you get every contract, it'll force you into late delivery penalties."

"No, you won't." Riley might not like Shane, but it seemed Shane stuck to his own moral code. "If you were going to fight dirty, you'd have kept hold of the engine mounting brackets. Or at least charged me a mark-up."

"It's not the same thing."

"Yeah, it kinda is."

"I'm not backing off," said Shane.

"I'm going to keep growing," said Riley.

"Then we're going to keep fighting."

"I thought we'd agreed to ignore each other."

"You want to sit here and scowl at each other instead?"

"Sure."

"We found a Chateau de Fontaines," Darci called out, breezing back into the room. "Kalissa's bringing you a glass," she said to Riley.

"We should take off," said Shane.

Darci glanced between the two men. She obviously understood the undercurrents, but she was doing her best to keep things light and cheerful.

"Early morning," Shane said to her, his tone implacable.

"You're right," she agreed easily.

"I think the corkscrew ran out of batteries," Kalissa said laughingly as she re-entered the room.

"We're going to say goodnight," Darci told her, moving to give her a quick hug.

Shane followed suit, hugging Kalissa tightly.

Riley found himself rising to his feet. He knew he had no cause to be jealous, but he hated watching another man touch her.

They finally made it out the door, and Kalissa returned her attention to the wine bottle, her tone still chirpy. "I'm not sure how we're going to break into this."

"*What are you doing?*" he asked.

"Huh?" she looked up.

"Is that all it takes? Expensive wine, free steak and crab?" Her expression fell. "What's the matter with you?"

"You can see what he's doing, can't you?" Riley advanced on her.

"Helping me out?"

"Throwing luxury in your face and hoping you'll like it."

"You want me to hate Chateau de Fontaines?"

"I brought beer. You used to like beer."

"Who says I don't like beer?"

Voices sounded down the hallway, and Riley remembered Megan and Garrison were still there.

"I also brought pizza, ordinary, normal, inexpensive pizza."

"Are you hungry?" she asked.

"I am."

"Then eat some pizza, and quit yelling at me."

"I'm not yelling at you." He stopped and lowered his voice. "I'm not yelling at you."

"You told me to come live here, Riley. You told me to do whatever Shane said."

"He's trying to steal you from me."

"No, he's not. He's already got my sister."

"Not like that."

"Then, like what?"

"He can't stand me."

"Well, you are trying to steal all his customers."

"It's more than that. He can't stand the fact that I'm breathing."

Kalissa set down the wine bottle.

"Grab the beer," she told him, reaching for the top button on her blouse.

"What are you—"

"Bring the pizza," she said, popping another button and another.

Riley glanced down the hall, worried about Garrison reappearing.

"Let's go be ordinary." She shrugged out of her blouse and let it drop to the floor.

"Stop it." He rushed forward.

She reached back to unclip her bra.

He grabbed her hand. "Seriously. Stop it."

"You want to fight with me?"

"No."

"Then bring the beer and the pizza." She tugged her hand away and sauntered down the hall to the first door. She opened it, slipped off her bra, and dropped the lacy garment on the hall floor, turning into the room.

Riley couldn't decide whether to be angry or amused. He was definitely aroused. Wasting no time, he balanced the beer and pizza in one hand, scooped up her blouse, then grabbed her bra and closed the bedroom door behind him.

"It locks," she told him, standing there in nothing but her panties.

"That's good." He quickly emptied his hands.

"This whole thing is confusing for me." She looked incredibly vulnerable standing nearly naked in the soft light.

"It must be," he said, moving instinctively toward her.

"I don't know how I'm supposed to act, what I'm supposed to feel."

"I want to help," he told her honestly.

"It's funny," she said, half to herself. "Right now, you're the most normal thing in my world."

He unbuttoned his shirt, tossing it away as he drew to a stop in front of her. "You're the most precious thing in mine."

She gave him a little smile. "You still want pizza?"

He kicked off his shoes. "Pizza can wait."

"It'll get cold."

"I'm getting hot."

Her smile grew. "I'm hot, too."

"You are definitely that." He reached out to cradle her head, stepping in.

"Riley?"

"Yeah?"

Their bodies met, meshing together as if they belonged like that.

"I didn't realize I was yours to steal."

"Surprised me, too." He leaned down to kiss her. "But I know that you are."

Twelve

Kalissa was slowly accepting that her life no longer had a normal.

"I'm clipping the transmitter to the back of your dress," the female technician told her. "It'll feel a bit clunky, but we'll keep it out of the camera angles."

"Have you ever done this before?" Kalissa asked Darci.

"Once," said Darci. "Under much more stressful circumstances."

"You don't find this stressful?"

They'd spent an hour in hair and makeup, had their black dresses fussed over by wardrobe, and now at least a dozen sound technicians, camera operators and assorted television crew were rushing around them on the stage.

Marion Ward, the local talk show anchor had briefly introduced herself, and then rushed off for her own preparations. Shane was standing in the wings, while Garrison and his cohorts were prowling around the studio, presumably checking for hidden dangers. The only thing frightening Kalissa at the moment was the idea of live television.

"It's better doing it live," said Darci. "That way, they can't selectively edit and make you sound stupid."

"I was hoping they could selectively edit to make me sound smart."

The technician smiled as she attached the mic to Kalissa's neckline.

"You're going to do fine," she told her.

"I'm going to freeze up."

"Then I'll do the talking," said Darci.

"Maybe we should have dressed exactly the same," said Kalissa. "That way, you could play both parts."

The technician chuckled.

Kalissa was wearing a form fitting black dress with cap

sleeves and a sweetheart neckline. Darci had also gone with black, but hers had spaghetti straps, beading on the bodice, and a short, pleated crepe skirt. Kalissa's hair was swirled up in a casual, messy knot, while Darci's was neatly braided above her forehead, flowing long down her back.

"Two minutes," called the producer.

Marion Ward rushed in, taking the high seat in between the two women. She sat straight, squared her shoulders, shifted at a slight angle to the camera, braced one foot on the cross bar and crossed her legs.

Kalissa watched carefully, emulating the pose, trying desperately to look relaxed.

"Let your shoulders drop," the sound tech whispered.

Then someone from hair and makeup rushed across the stage, fixing the hair at Kalissa's temple.

"Sixty seconds."

"First question is about your father," Marion said to Darci.

Darci nodded. She looked poised and confident.

Kalissa was starting to sweat.

The producer counted down, and everyone on the stage went still and quiet. The red lights came on for each of the three cameras.

"Three, two, one."

"Good evening, Chicago," Marion sang out. "And Welcome to City Shore Beat. With me tonight is Colborn Aerospace billionaire, Darci Colborn."

Kalissa's mouth twitched for a second. She felt an urge to correct the statement and say that Darci was now only a quarter billionaire.

"You'll remember her from this summer's grand wedding to Shane Colborn." Marion turned to Darci. "Welcome to the show."

"Happy to be here," Darci said with an easy smile.

"And joining us, to the shock and surprise of everyone in Chicago, including Darci Colborn, is Darci's identical twin sister, Kalissa Smith."

Two of the cameras swung to Kalissa. She fixed a smile on her face.

"Welcome to the show, Kalissa."

"Thank you," Kalissa managed.

"This is a tale of scandal, betrayal and long-lost sisters reunited."

Kalissa glanced to Shane while she struggled to keep her expression neutral. This didn't sound promising.

He gave her a thumb's up.

Marion canted her body toward Darci. "Darci, I understand you were raised by your father."

"I was. Ian Rivers was a brilliant if underappreciated engineer and innovator."

Marion turned to Kalissa. "You were separated at birth. Put up for adoption. You never knew your parents or your twin sister."

Kalissa wasn't sure there was a question in there. "Yes," she said.

"As far as we can tell," Darci jumped in. "Our parents separated, each planning to raise one of us. Unfortunately, our birth mother passed away when Kalissa was just a toddler."

Marion returned to Darci, obviously deciding she was going to be the better guest.

Kalissa wanted to apologize. But more than that, she wanted to run off the stage. Instead, she did her best to smile, knowing one of the cameras had stayed focused on her.

"But Kalissa wasn't returned to her father?"

"We don't know all the details," Darci said smoothly. "We do know our father was a business partner with Dalton Colborn. That's how Shane and I met. We've also learned, unbeknownst to my husband, that our father, Ian Rivers, was pivotal in creating the technology used by Colborn Aerospace today as a leading producer of commercial jets."

Kalissa cracked her first real smile. Shane had bet Darci she wouldn't find a way to plug the company.

"Shane and I were thrilled to meet Kalissa. She only learned of my existence because of our recent wedding. As

I'm sure has happened with many families, we were reunited because of pictures broadcast on the Internet."

Marion turned back to Kalissa. "What was your first reaction? How did you feel when you saw Darci for the first time?"

"I thought it was a joke," Kalissa answered honestly. "I thought somebody had photo shopped my face into her wedding pictures."

"And when you found out it was true? That your birth sister was one of the richest people in the country?"

Kalissa hesitated again. There was a calculating look in Marion's eyes. She was definitely setting up for the gold-digger angle, and Kalissa didn't know how to deflect it.

Darci spoke up. "My sister did the most honorable and unexpected thing."

A fleeting look of frustration crossed Marion's face. But then she smiled, and switched to Darci. "Which was?"

"She came to warn me. She had a date that night, and she was afraid people would mistake her for me, and that I'd be embarrassed by it. Shane and I were grateful."

"Grateful in a monetary sense?" asked Marion.

Kalissa was getting concerned. This was supposed to be a friendly interview.

"Are you asking if I've taken any of their money?" asked Kalissa.

Marion swung toward her. "Have you?"

"We've tried very hard to support Kalissa," said Darci. "But she's incredibly independent. The important thing for us is that we've found each other again and reunited as a family."

"That's the important thing," agreed Kalissa.

"But it's vastly changed your circumstances in life," Marion prompted, gesturing toward Kalissa.

"Vastly," Kalissa admitted. "But I imagine that's the case for everyone who finds a long lost relative, whether they're rich or not. I want people to know that I'm not Darci, and Darci's not me. There are two of us, and we look alike." Kalissa stared directly into the camera. "So, if you come across one of us, and we're doing something undignified or inappropriate, assume that it's me. As you can probably tell from this interview, my sister is much more sophisticated than I am. I'm about five minutes out of thrift stores and burger joints."

"Did I mention she has a terrific sense of humor?" asked Darci. Then she unexpectedly came out of her chair, crossing the stage in front of Marion.

Her move seemed to cause a flurry of activity behind the cameras, and Marion appeared quite horrified.

But, Darci kept walking, opening her arms to Kalissa. "Thank goodness you found us." Then she pulled her into a tight hug.

Ducking around Darci, Marion found a new camera angle. "And, uh, we'll be right back."

Darci drew back and gave Marion a withering look. "We're done." She unclipped her mic.

Shane was with them in seconds, followed by the security team.

"Clear the stage," ordered the producer.

A sound technician helped Darci scramble out of the microphone set up, and she quickly followed Shane and Darci out of the studio. Garrison walked beside her.

"What happened?" she asked. She realized it hadn't gone as they'd expected, but she wasn't sure why Darci was angry.

"You didn't need to say all that about yourself," said Garrison.

Kalissa didn't see it that way. "I just told the truth. That woman wasn't letting us say what we came to say."

"There was nothing in particular you needed to say. You only needed to be seen together. That host boxed you into a corner. It made Darci mad."

"I want the world to know it's me and not Darci out there making mistakes."

"You're not making mistakes, ma'am."

"You can call me Kalissa, you know."

"Not on the job."

"You call Megan by her first name."

There was a split second's hesitation before he spoke. "I'm not assigned to protect Megan."

They passed through the exterior door into the studio parking lot. Kalissa's eyes adjusted to the sunlight, and she immediately spotted Riley. He was thirty yards away, leaning against his sports car.

"Riley?" she said out loud. "What is he—" She stepped away from the group, walking toward him.

He straightened to meet her and smiled.

"What are you doing here?" she asked.

"I wanted to make sure it went okay."

"Why didn't you come inside?"

His gaze moved beyond her to Darci and the rest of the group. "It seemed like a family thing."

"It didn't go so well," she told him.

"I saw. I watched the broadcast on-line."

Kalissa nodded. "Garrison says I should have kept my mouth shut and just sat there."

"In those exact words?" Riley asked.

"Not exactly. But Darci cut it off because I was blowing it."

He took her hand. "You want to walk?" He nodded toward a walkway and an open green space along the curve of the river.

Kalissa glanced back at the group. "Garrison will have to come with us."

"Don't worry about Garrison. It's his job to worry about you."

"I don't want to make his job harder."

"You won't. It's not. Stop worrying about everyone else." He called out to the others. "We'll meet you back at the penthouse."

Kalissa decided some fresh air would do her good. She'd been cooped up in the apartment for four days now, and she needed to clear her head.

She walked beside Riley, putting the interview from her mind, forgetting about Garrison and everyone else. Trains and traffic echoed against skyscrapers across the water, boats chugged past, and they joined the steady stream of pedestrians taking in the afternoon.

Part of her wanted to tell him about her father and the inheritance. But another part wanted to keep the secret inside. It felt like, once she told him, the last barrier to her new reality would be gone. She wasn't ready yet.

They turned to walk along the black railing. A breeze swirled up from the water, chilling the air.

Riley shrugged out of his jacket and draped it around her shoulders.

"I've been thinking," she said.

"That's good."

"About taking Shane up on his offer."

"What offer is that?" She could hear the hesitation in Riley's words.

"Landscaping the mansion. Me and Megan. It would keep us working, keep our regular crews busy, but it would keep me out of the public eye."

Once it became known she was a shareholder in Colborn Aerospace, Kalissa knew her days of wheeling bark mulch and azalea shrubs would have to end. But she couldn't imagine being qualified to do anything for Colborn Aerospace.

"I'm sure Shane would like that." There was an edge to Riley's voice. "The place is a fortress."

"Garrison would like that," Kalissa joked, not wanting the conversation to get negative.

She glanced behind them to see where he was.

"I told you not to worry about Garrison. He knows his job. He seems good at it. You just have to live your life."

Kalissa couldn't help but laugh at that statement. She didn't even understand her life, never mind know how to live it anymore. She stopped walking, turning to lean on the rail and gaze out.

"What do you like about me?" she asked him.

He linked his arm with hers. "Everything."

"I mean specifically."

"Specifically, I like everything about you."

She sighed. "I feel like I'm caught between two worlds. One I know, and in it I'm doing okay. The other is unfamiliar and kind of scary, and I don't know if I can succeed."

"You'll be fine," he said, but she knew he didn't understand the magnitude of the problem.

"I'm going to change. I'll have to change. But I was thinking. If I knew the best parts of me, I could make sure I kept them."

He faced her and smiled. "You're not going to lose the best parts of you. They're you. They'll go anywhere and everywhere you go."

"I can't do my job anymore. I can't dig up people's front yards, lay stone and push wheelbarrow loads of manure."

"You can still do the planning. That's mostly your part anyway. Have you ever actually laid any stone? And when's the last time you dumped manure?"

"You know what I mean."

"I do," he said, putting his hand over hers. "Tell me what I can do to help?"

"This," she said. "Today. One more day. Can we go back to the pier, buy ourselves a corndog and be incredibly ordinary for a while?"

He brought her hand to his lips and gave her knuckles a tender kiss. "We can do anything you want."

To Riley, the Colborn mansion felt like the lion's den.

He followed a butler through what he knew to be the grand hall. Used mostly for entertaining, it had soaring, twenty foot ceilings, marble pillars and gleaming white archways. Around the perimeter were antique style lampposts, with an ostentatious wrought iron chandelier hanging in the center of the room.

Riley could only imagine who they were trying to impress. In the center of the room, a bronze stallion statue was perched on a massive, hewn wood table. Oil paintings hung on the walls, Dalton, Shane's mother, Shane himself.

Riley slowed down to look at them.

"If you'd care to wait here," said the butler, gesturing to a grouping of walnut and red velvet armchairs. "I'll find Ms. Smith."

Riley wasn't sure if it was a question or a command, so he nodded. One room in this place was as bad as another.

The butler's footfalls faded slowly away on the hardwood floor while Riley gazed at the paintings. He took in a suit of armor and some bronze statuettes placed on heavy, wooden tables. He couldn't help but wonder how often his mother had polished the pieces. They looked like they'd been there for decades.

He gazed around the huge room, mentally comparing it to their small, basement apartment twenty miles away. His mother had ridden two buses every day to get here. She'd cleaned up after Dalton Colborn, his wife and their guests, growing tired and ill while Dalton had looked down his nose at her, never caring that she'd once shared his bed.

The sound of footsteps echoed behind him, and he turned, expecting Kalissa.

It was Shane, who stopped short, obviously surprised to see Riley.

The two stared at each other, while resentment churned in Riley's gut.

Then Shane walked forward. "I didn't know you were here."

"I didn't expect you either."

It was midday Thursday, and Riley had guessed Shane would still be in the city.

"Starting the weekend early," said Shane. "You?"

"I'm here to see Kalissa." Riley stated the obvious.

"She's outside."

"Your butler told me to wait here."

Shane gave an absent nod, his gaze going to the large portrait of Dalton directly above them. Riley couldn't help but wonder if Shane was also considering the irony.

"I bet he'd turn over in his grave," said Riley.

Shane's gaze narrowed, but Riley wasn't in the mood to back off.

"Seeing you and me, here, together."

"Why?" asked Shane.

"Please don't," said Riley, his stomach cramping, his tone going hard. "Not here. Not now. Not when it's just you and me."

"Don't ask a question?"

"Don't play dumb," Riley spat out.

But Shane wouldn't let up. "He'd hate Ellis Aviation?"

"Yeah, right. Ellis Aviation is what would tick him off."

"Okay," said Shane, evidently willing to let it drop.

Well Riley wasn't, not this time, not if he was going to continue to see Kalissa and keep running into Shane. Not next to the antiques his mother hand polished, under Dalton's roof, with Shane standing there as the new lord of the manor.

"I'm talking about me," said Riley. "He'd hate *me*." He waited for Shane's reaction.

"Are you saying he knew you?"

Now they were getting somewhere.

"My mother brought me here once. I was thirteen. I was just old enough to get it. Do you know what he said? Do you know what he said to his own son?"

Shane went still.

Yeah, Riley had said it. He'd spoken the forbidden words the mighty Colborn family had hidden for so long. "He said, 'servants use the back door, and they don't wear dirty shoes in the hall'."

Shane reached out and braced himself on a table.

"That was it," said Riley. "The only words our old man ever uttered to me, and the only time he ever looked at me."

"He didn't—"

"Don't make excuses for him," Riley ground out. "You resent Ellis Aviation? You don't like me touching your sister-in-law? You think you can keep the Colborn family untainted by the illegitimate son of a *servant*?" Once rolling, Riley barely stopped for breath.

"I know you're poisoning Kalissa against me," he ground out. "And it's not going to work. I won't let it work. I grew up tough, Shane, a whole lot tougher than you. I was on the outside, and it was cold out there. I watched him dote on you. I watched him tutor you. Then I watched him hand you his world on a silver platter. All the while, I was fighting down there in the dirt. You might hate me, but that's nothing compared to how I feel about you."

The color had drained from Shane's face, and his chest rapidly rose and fell.

"Riley?" Kalissa shocked voice was directly behind them.

Riley pivoted, his stomach bottoming out, while Shane stood frozen.

"Riley?" she repeated. "*What* is going on?"

He cursed a streak inside his brain.

She swallowed. "Is it true? It's true," she laughed a little hysterically.

"I'm sorry," he blurted out, moving toward her.

She recoiled, taking a step back.

"I wanted to tell you." He kicked himself for letting his temper get away from him.

"That you're Shane's brother? His *brother*?" The pitch of her voice went higher. Her hand went to her forehead as if she had a sudden pain. "That you hate and resent him?"

"This is bad," said Riley. "I never would have—"

"Bad doesn't begin to describe it." She took another backward step. "I see it now. It's been about this all along."

He moved, trying to keep the distance small between them. "I shouldn't have come here. It was stupid for me to come here. I thought I could handle…"

"The lies?" she asked.

"I didn't lie."

"You did *nothing* but lie."

"Ellis," said Shane.

"Not now," Riley barked over his shoulder.

Kalissa let out a whimper and turned on her heel.

Riley followed, but she began to run.

"Ellis," Shane called behind him.

Riley ignored him. He had to get to Kalissa.

He caught up to her in the main reception room. She was heading for a staircase.

"Kalissa, *stop*."

She stopped. But she didn't turn around.

He slowed his pace, coming up behind her. "I know this must be a shock. I didn't say anything, because—"

"I'm only stopping because I want this to be final. I know I've been an easy mark. I don't know why, but I was attracted to you." She gave an unsteady laugh. Still, she kept her back to him. "You obviously know I was attracted to you. But I know how you operate, solidify your position before revealing the truth. It's not going to work a second time. I can't help you compete with your brother. I can't help you be a Colborn."

Riley was horrified by the statement. "That's not what I want."

She turned, finally. "Yes, it is." Her eyes glistened with tears.

"You and me, we have nothing to do with the Colborns."

"We have *everything* to do with the Colborns. Shane's the reason you want me. Dalton's the reason you're here. Your past drives you. From what I can see, it's always driven you." She swallowed and seemed to force herself to moderate her voice. "At least now I know why. I understand you, Riley."

"No, you don't."

She didn't understand him. If she understood him, she'd know he was in love with her.

"Leave," she said. "Just leave."

"I can't."

"You don't have a choice."

"Let's go somewhere, anywhere but here. Let's talk this through. I never, *ever* meant for any of this to hurt you."

She gave a weak smile. "So you can lie to me some more."

"I'm not going to lie. There's nothing left. You know everything."

She paused. "Yes, I do. I know everything. Goodbye, Riley."

"Kalissa, no."

But she was mounting the stairs.

He could see Garrison out of the corner of his eye. Riley wanted to chase her. But he knew he'd never get there. Garrison wouldn't let him get near her.

He tried to reason with her. "How can talking hurt?"

But she didn't stop, she didn't even look, she just disappeared around the corner of the staircase.

Riley's heart was pumping. It took every last ounce of control that he had to remain at the bottom of those stairs. There had to be something he could do. He needed a next move. But he couldn't for the life of him come up with one.

"Riley," Shane called out, passing Garrison to approach him.

"Not now," said Riley. "*Not…now.*"

He knew leaving was his only move. Leaving and regrouping, then coming back, coming at this from another angle. Because there was no way this was the end for him and Kalissa.

Kalissa made her way across the mansion on the second floor. She took the service stairs and left through the back exit. There, she found Megan in the rose garden.

"I know it's a few weeks before we can start," said Megan, smiling with what looked like pure joy. "But I can't help wandering around out here and salivating. There's so much we can do with these grounds."

Kalissa forced her own smile. "Do you know where you want to start?"

"Not yet. Maybe the pond. How fun would it be to expand and get some pure white swans."

"Sure. Swans."

"I'm joking, of course." Megan peered at her. "Kalissa? What's wrong?"

"Nothing. Well. I just broke up with Riley." Kalissa's legs suddenly lost all their strength, and she sat down on the grass.

"You what?" Megan crouched down beside her. "Why? What happened?"

"Kalissa?" Darci called from the lawn beyond the garden.

"Over here," Megan answered, sitting down next to Kalissa. "Does she know?"

Kalissa nodded, her chest heavy and aching. "Shane was there."

Darci rushed past the Pink Flamingo bushes. "Are you all right?" she asked, dropping down beside Kalissa and giving her shoulders a squeeze. "I'm so, so sorry."

"What happened?" asked Megan.

"Riley lied again. Or is it still. I think it's still."

"Shane had no idea," said Darci. "He's stunned."

"What did he lie about?" asked Megan, glancing from one woman to the other.

"He's Shane's brother," said Kalissa. She reached out and grasped Megan's arm. She was coming clean, here and now. "And I'm inheriting—" She looked to Darci. "Is that the right way to say it? Inheriting?"

"Say it however you want."

"Part of Colborn Aerospace," Kalissa finished.

"What?" Megan looked confused.

"I'm not keeping any more secrets. I was trying to wrap my head around it, but you need to know. I tried to stop it, but I couldn't. It looks like I'm going to be crazy rich."

"What does that have to do with Riley?" asked Megan.

"Nothing," said Kalissa. "He doesn't know." Then it dawned on her. "I guess I'm keeping secrets from him, too." It was comically ironic.

"It's not the same thing," said Darci.

"Am I wrong?" asked Kalissa. "Was I wrong to keep quiet?"

"You broke up with him?" asked Megan. "Or the other way around?"

"It was me," said Kalissa. "He was talking to Shane, yelling at Shane really. He's spent his entire life wanting what Shane has, maybe even wanting to *be* Shane."

"So, Dalton was his father?" Megan asked. "He had a different mother?"

"She worked here," said Darci. "Apparently she was one of the housekeepers."

"Riley said she was young and didn't want to lose her job," said Kalissa, battling against instinctive sympathy for Riley. "That was before I knew he was talking about Dalton Colborn and this particular mansion."

"Shane didn't know," said Darci. "Riley thinks Shane shunned him all these years. But he didn't know."

"That had to be tough on Riley," said Megan.

"I can't help feeling sorry for him," said Kalissa.

She wanted to stay angry, but she couldn't help picturing him as a young boy, a teenager. He was hurt, wounded, and it seemed to have impacted his entire life.

"Maybe it's too soon to ask," said Darci. "Could you ever forgive Riley?"

Kalissa wanted it to be that simple. Her throat closed over again. "It's not about that. It's about Shane. Whatever Shane has, Riley wants, too. He's not thinking clearly. He's not seeing me clearly. It's all emotion and dark history." Darci's face twisted in a grimace. "He wanted me before he came anywhere close to knowing me." Kalissa looked to Megan for confirmation.

Megan didn't disagree.

"He had tunnel vision the whole time," said Kalissa. "And I was flattered. It was hard not to be flattered."

"But you like him, too," said Darci.

"Are you on his side?" Megan asked.

"I don't want there to be sides."

"Because he's Shane's brother," Kalissa finished for her. It was a terrible situation for Darci and Shane. Kalissa started to rise. "Listen, I'm going to get out of the way—"

"You're not going *anywhere*," said Darci, grasping Kalissa's elbow.

"This is a disaster." A tear crept from Kalissa's eye.

"And we're going to figure it out together," said Darci.

"I can't see him. I won't see him."

"You don't have to see anyone. I'm on your side, now and always. You're my family."

"Riley is Shane's family."

"It's not the same thing," said Darci.

"How is it different?"

"I don't know, but it is."

"I'm going to hate him," said Kalissa, trying, but failing to be strong.

The upright posture lasted about twenty seconds before she slumped. "Maybe tomorrow. I can start hating him tomorrow."

Darci slipped her arm around Kalissa's shoulders. "We just have to make it to tomorrow."

Kalissa gave a gloomy nod. Tomorrow seemed incredibly far away.

"We'll do something fun," Darci said with encouragement.

Kalissa knew she was reaching. She was trying to be a good sister, and come up with a distraction.

"Like what?" asked Megan, gamely buying in.

"Dinner out, somewhere nice?"

"I'm not going out in public," said Kalissa. That was the last thing she wanted to do.

"A tour of the wine cellar?" Darci suggested.

Getting drunk was tempting, but Kalissa knew she'd only feel worse in the morning. "Pass."

"Well, that's disappointing," said Megan with a mock pout.

Darci shrugged. "Wine cellar's not going anywhere. We'll do that another day." Then she snapped her fingers. "I've got it. Spa day. Well spa night. Night and day. There's no rush to get back."

"No, thanks," said Kalissa. "I don't want to run into anyone who saw the broadcast."

"We won't." Darci's voice held a lot of conviction. "Not in upstate New York."

Both Kalissa and Megan gaped at her in confusion.

"I've got a jet," explained Darci, pulling out her phone.

It took Megan a moment to speak. "You mean a private jet?"

"There's a place called Glimmer Mist Falls. Massage, facial, pedicure, mineral springs. They'll send a limo to meet the plane."

Kalissa shook her head. She just wanted to bury herself under the covers and wait for unconsciousness.

Megan stuck her hand in the air. "I'm in."

"We're not taking no for an answer," said Darci. "Garrison will help."

Kalissa had no desire to go along. Then again, she wasn't sure she had the energy to fight them off either.

"Sweetheart?" Darci said into the phone. "We want to take the jet to Glimmer Mist Falls." Her gaze went to Kalissa, turning sympathetic. "I think so, too." She paused. "We will. Thanks, honey."

Thirteen

For the next three days, Riley focused on two things, work at Ellis Aviation and coming up with a strategy to win back Kalissa. The work part was easy. All he needed there was energy and an edge. His frustration gave him both.

Getting Kalissa back seemed impossible. As long as she was out at the mansion, he couldn't get near her. He knew Shane would keep the place locked down tight. And Garrison was loyal to Shane. He might sympathize with Riley, but he would definitely do his job.

Even if Riley could find a way to see her, he didn't know what he'd say. She was right to accuse him of lying. He hadn't told her about Shane. And that made it look like Shane mattered. He didn't.

He cracked open a bottle of whisky in his kitchen, pouring a couple of ounces over ice. Liquor might not be the answer. But he was tired, and it was late, and he was sick of dreaming about Kalissa.

The dreams were spectacular, but waking up was a nightmare.

A knock sounded on his front door.

He double checked the clock. It was coming up on ten. While Ashton might drop in this late, Ashton was on his way to Alaska today. He'd invited Riley along. Riley had to admit, he'd been tempted.

He crossed to the foyer and opened the door, shocked to find Shane on the front porch.

"Is Kalissa all right?" The question was out before Riley could censor it.

"She's fine," said Shane. "She's in New York."

For some reason, the answer struck Riley as absurd. "Why is she in New York?"

All this time, he'd been picturing her at the mansion. It

annoyed him to be wrong. It annoyed him more that it was Shane who had the information.

"Darci took her to a spa. Garrison's with them."

"She's been wanting a spa day," said Riley, wondering why he was bothering to make small talk.

"You mind if I come in?" asked Shane.

The answer was yes. But fighting with Shane seemed like a reasonable distraction. So he stepped back. "Why not."

Shane entered, and Riley closed the door behind him.

"Drink?" asked Riley, holding up his glass.

"Yeah."

Riley headed for the kitchen, and Shane followed.

He poured another whisky, not particularly caring if it was Shane's preference or not. Then he handed Shane the glass.

"Why are you here?"

"Right to the point," said Shane. He took a swallow.

"No reason to beat around the bush. Do you want me to close my company? Leave the state? Have you changed your mind about fighting dirty?"

"I didn't know," said Shane.

"Didn't know what?"

"That Dalton was your father. That you were my brother."

"The hell you didn't," said Riley. "We talked about it."

Shane drew back, showing an admirable display of amazement. "When?"

"Freshman year, high school baseball tournament. We were on opposite teams."

Shane's gaze went off into space. "I have no recollection of anything like that."

"I called you brother and said we should talk. You called me a loser and a twerp and told me to get lost."

Shane seemed speechless.

Riley finished his drink and poured another.

"I couldn't have understood," said Shane.

"Right," said Riley. "It's your story. Tell it however you want."

"Honestly," said Shane. "I didn't understand. I didn't know. You think I'd *ignore* that all these years?"

"You did."

Shane paced across the kitchen. "I didn't. I don't know what else to say. Did my dad know?"

Riley set the bottle down with a crack. "She begged him to help her. He agreed not to fire her."

Shane swore angrily. He swallowed the whisky then marched over and poured himself another. "That's why Ellis Aviation."

Riley didn't argue the point.

"I can't say I blame you," said Shane. "Have you done DNA? Why didn't you come after some of his money? Even Darci came after his money."

"I'm not Darci."

"Fair enough. So, what do you want?"

Riley didn't even have to think about that. "Kalissa."

"I mean from me."

"You've got her right now."

Shane seemed to ponder. "I don't see that happening."

"I don't see me giving up."

"I don't think I can let you hurt her anymore."

Riley set down the new drink. He really wasn't thirsty anymore. "I never wanted to hurt her."

"So you keep claiming. Yet, it keeps on happening." Shane snagged a kitchen chair, setting it backward and straddling it. "I have a proposition for you."

Riley folded his arms over his chest and braced himself against the counter.

"Half," said Shane. "Right down the middle. The DNA checks out, you get half of my interest in Colborn Aerospace, half ownership of the mansion. I'm keeping the penthouse, but I'm sure you can afford your own. And I'll publicly acknowledge you, tell the world you're Dalton's son."

"Very funny," said Riley, battling to keep his emotions in check. He couldn't afford to take Shane seriously on this.

"It's not a joke," said Shane.

"What's the catch?"

"Catch is…"

Riley waited for it.

"You leave Kalissa alone."

"No." The word all but leapt from Riley's soul.

"That's my condition."

"The answer is no."

Shane rested his arm on the back of the chair. "Whether you mean to or not, you hurt her. Hurting her, hurts Darci, and I will do anything to protect Darci."

"Including buying off your illegitimate brother?"

Riley's emotions settled to normal levels. Yeah, this was Shane's idea of a joke all right, toss him an offer he couldn't accept.

"Including that," said Shane.

"Forget it."

"You're saying no to a quarter billion?"

"The price is too high."

Shane came to his feet. "For Kalissa."

"I want her back."

Shane returned the chair and moved to stand in front of Riley. "I'll hire an army."

"I know you will."

The two men stared at each other.

"You know," said Shane. "You look a little like him."

"I don't take that as a compliment."

Shane squinted. "I think we both know what the DNA is going to say."

"It's irrelevant."

"Maybe." Shane stepped back and started out of the kitchen. In the doorway, he turned back. "For the record, that was a good answer."

"For the record," Riley called to Shane's retreating back. "I couldn't give a crap what any Colborn thinks of me."

He reached for the glass and polished off the second drink.

Kalissa followed Darci up the compact staircase into the Colborn jet. They'd spent four days at the Glimmer Mist Falls spa, and she told herself she felt better. Megan had returned to Chicago after the first day to finish up Mosaic's final jobs, but Darci had insisted Kalissa stay.

Kalissa hadn't been inclined to argue. She was missing Riley every minute, and she hadn't been able to bear the thought of returning to the mansion or the penthouse. She wasn't sure she could do it now, but she knew she couldn't stay away forever.

The co-pilot greeted them in the doorway, cheerfully welcoming them on board. Despite several massages and dips in the mineral pool, Kalissa's muscles felt stiff and sore. She was trying to snap out of it, but her body felt heavy, and her head felt like it was packed in cotton.

"Darling?" said Darci as she entered the plane, a note of surprise in her voice.

Kalissa passed by the co-pilot to see Shane standing between the seats in the front row.

"I came along for the ride," he said, kissing Darci and giving her a quick squeeze. "Hi, Kalissa."

Kalissa mustered a smile. "Hi, Shane."

"How are you doing?" he asked, gesturing for Darci to take the window in a grouping of four seats around a small table.

"I'm fine," Kalissa automatically answered, moving to the seat facing Darci.

Shane looked to Darci for confirmation.

Darci made a rocking motion with the flat of her hand.

"I'm better than I was," Kalissa insisted.

"Marginally," said Darci. "I seriously thought about staying another day."

"We can't," said Kalissa.

"You can if you want," said Shane. He looked to Darci.

"I want to get back," said Kalissa, telling herself she meant it.

She'd sat around long enough wallowing in self-pity. People got through heartbreak all the time. She'd do it, too.

"Are you ready, sir?" asked the co-pilot.

"We're ready," said Shane.

The co-pilot secured the door, and they all buckled up.

"Thank you for doing this," Kalissa told Darci. Then her gaze took in Shane as well. "To both of you."

"You don't have to thank us," said Shane. "The money, this plane, even the mansion are yours now as much as they are ours."

She'd heard it from Darci a dozen times. But this time, Kalissa didn't let herself argue. It was time to accept her new life. In fact, it was time to embrace her new life.

"I want to know how to help," she said to Shane. "I can't just renovate the grounds forever. I want to contribute to the company."

Shane smiled. "Good for you."

As the plane taxied toward the runway, Kalissa squared her shoulders, feeling ever so slightly lighter.

"What about interior design?" asked Darci. "You've got a flair for color and pattern, and you definitely have an eye for utility."

"You mean, pick out upholstery colors and carpets?" asked Kalissa.

"She means head up the interior design division," said Shane.

"She could job shadow Agnes for a few months," Darci said to Shane. Then she switched to Kalissa. "Agnes is retiring at the beginning of next year. We have to find her a replacement."

"Maybe," said Kalissa, wondering how she could possibly be qualified.

The engines revved up to full power, and the captain released the brakes, sending them rushing down the runway. The jet was light and powerful, and it took off quickly, climbing up over the small town and banking along the river.

"I went to see Riley yesterday," said Shane as they leveled off.

Darci looked at Shane in surprise, while Kalissa stilled. Her chest tightened up again.

"Do we need to talk about that right now, sweetheart?" Darci put a wealth of meaning into her tone.

Shane seemed to ignore his wife. "I have to ask you, Kalissa."

"No, you don't," said Darci. "You don't have to ask her anything right now."

"What?" asked Kalissa. She was angry and heartsick, but she still found herself thirsty for news of Riley. She was in love with an illusion, and it was pathetic.

"I made him an offer," said Shane.

"Of what?" asked Darci, starting to sound exasperated.

Shane kept his focus on Kalissa. "Public acknowledgement that he's my brother and half of my interest in Colborn Aerospace. Plus, rights to the mansion."

"*What*?" Darci all but jumped out of her seat. "Why would you *make him part of our lives*?"

Kalissa had the same question, but it was none of her business, and she wasn't sure she could speak right now anyway. Riley tied up with Colborn? Riley coming and going from the mansion? There was no way she could cope with it.

But where could she go? Maybe leave Chicago?

"There was one condition," said Shane, his voice calm and steady. "He walks away from Kalissa. He doesn't hurt her by trying to get her back."

"You bought him off?" asked Darci. She glanced worriedly at Kalissa.

If possible, Kalissa felt even sicker. By lying to her and breaking her heart, Riley had convinced Shane to give him everything he ever wanted.

He'd won, and she'd lost her heart.

"He turned it down," said Shane.

"What part?" asked Darci, clearly confused.

"All parts," said Shane. "Everything. He refused to give up Kalissa. He said his birthright and a quarter billion weren't enough."

Darci's mouth opened, but she didn't say anything.

There was a roaring sound in Kalissa's ears. It seemed like the jet engine was getting louder and louder and louder.

"Kalissa?" Darci prompted, reaching to take her hand.

"I don't—" was all Kalissa managed.

"He picked you over me. He picked you over Colborn." Shane broke into a smile and gave what looked like an astonished shake of his head.

"Did he not understand the offer?"

"He understood," said Shane.

"Then why?" She couldn't form the right question. But she also couldn't stop a stubborn glimmer of hope.

"There's only one reason he'd do that," said Shane.

"Don't tell me you trust him," said Darci.

Kalissa found herself holding her breath.

"I don't know if I'd go that far," said Shane. "But I do know that he's in love with Kalissa."

"You're on *his* side?" asked Darci.

Shane gave an unabashed shrug. "He is my brother."

Kalissa's chest buzzed with a mixture of excitement and trepidation. She knew better than to hope, but she simply couldn't stop herself.

Riley stayed at the Ellis plant on Sunday until the walls started to close in. Then he headed to the gym, working out until he was exhausted, going home to a very long, hot shower.

He slipped on a pair of worn, gray sweats and padded barefoot into the kitchen, sticking his head in the fridge. He needed comfort food, maybe pizza or nachos or chocolate cake. He'd get lost in an action flick or three, then fall into bed and try very hard not to dream.

He knew he had to pick up the pieces of his life, but it wasn't going to happen tonight.

His front doorbell rang, and he swung the fridge door shut. He was torn between ignoring the sound and wishing it was something to distract him—maybe one of his neighbors was having a party or a flood.

It rang again, and he crossed through the living room to the foyer, opening the door.

His brain staggered to a stop.

Kalissa stood on his porch in a sophisticated, gold dress

with cap sleeves and a short skirt. Her hair was done up in a braid, and her makeup was heavier than usual.

"I bought this in New York," she said apologetically. "I'm a princess now, truly part of the Colborn empire."

"No. You're not." He didn't know what point she was making, but he knew it wasn't true.

"I've changed." There was a challenge in her voice.

"Not on the inside." He could see past anything she wore, any hairdo, any amount of makeup. "You'll always be you."

She moved through the doorway. Her expression seemed to relax, and she took in his damp hair, his bare chest and his bare feet.

He wanted to hope, but he didn't dare. Past her, he could see Garrison in the driveway. "Kalissa, what are you doing here?"

"We need to talk." She put a cool palm on his chest.

"Sure." He'd never refuse her, but he could already feel himself careening toward fresh heartbreak.

"But I don't want to talk." She tipped her chin, gazing up at him with the most blatantly sensual expression in her eyes.

"Kalissa." He was only going to be able to stand this for about five seconds.

"If you say the wrong thing." She brushed her body against his. "Then I'm going to have to walk out."

He wouldn't say the wrong thing. He *couldn't* say the wrong thing. He swung the door shut behind her.

"But if this is going to end," she said.

If? She'd said if. He clung to the word.

"Then I want to make love one more time."

She was talking nonsense. But he didn't care.

He scooped her into his arms, heading immediately for the bedroom. It was an outrageous suggestion. But he wasn't about to argue.

He set her on her feet next to his bed.

"Kalissa—"

"Don't," she whispered. She stretched up, pressing forward for a kiss.

He settled his lips on hers, raking his hand through her hair. But before it could get interesting, she broke away.

His heart sank.

But she stripped off her panties, tossing them aside. Then she yanked off his sweats and pressed down on his shoulders.

He sat on the bed. She slipped onto his lap, straddling his hips.

"Once fast," she told him. "Then again, really, really slow."

"Oh, yeah," he whispered, putting reason on hold and taking control of their kiss.

He made love to her twice over, communicating with nothing but touches, sighs and moans. Then when they were covered in sweat, and neither of them could move, he tucked her head against his shoulder and relaxed in complete satisfaction.

This had to be good. This couldn't be bad. Maybe they'd talk now, or maybe they'd wait until morning. Whichever it was, he had to get it right.

His phone rang.

He reached out and checked the number. "It's Garrison."

Kalissa smiled.

Riley answered. "Yeah?"

"Over to you?" Garrison asked.

"You can pick her up in the morning."

Kalissa stretched her arms above her head to grip the brass rails on his headboard.

Riley let his gaze scan her tempting body. "Maybe," he said to Garrison.

"Talk to you then," said Garrison.

"Yeah." Riley ended the call.

"This is a nice room," said Kalissa, gazing around at his furniture.

"You look very good in it." He wondered, if he barricaded the doors, how long it would take for someone to break in and rescue her.

"It's so normal," she said with a sigh. "Do you think we could stay here?"

"Yes." If he had his way, she was staying here forever.

She grinned, then sobered. "There's something I didn't tell you. And I'm sorry I didn't."

The statement surprised him. "You have a secret?"

She nodded. "It's about Colborn."

His phone rang again.

He swore.

"It could be Garrison."

"Don't move a muscle," said Riley. "You look perfect exactly the way you are."

He put one hand on her smooth stomach and used the other to pick up his phone. The number was blocked.

"Yeah?" His tone was impatient.

"Is Kalissa still with you?"

"Shane?"

"She's still there?"

"Absolutely," said Riley.

"Okay, so here's my new deal."

"Seriously? Do we have to do this *now*?"

"You keep Kalissa."

Riley stilled. He was listening.

"I publicly acknowledge you as my brother." Shane continued. "We merge Colborn and Ellis Aviation. We split the proceeds. We share the mansion. I'm still keeping the penthouse, but I figure you can share Kalissa's."

Riley wanted to scream the word *yes*! "Kalissa says she wants to stay here."

"Oh." Shane's tone turned cautious. "Well, I guess we can arrange something."

"Good."

"Have you proposed yet?"

"Goodbye, Shane."

"As your big brother, I feel it's my duty to—"

"You're a whole two months older than me."

"And a whole two months more married. Lock down the deal, bro. Do it now."

"I will," said Riley. He hesitated to ask the next question. "You think I have a chance?"

"A quarter billion is a lot of money. She knows you gave it up for her."

"Yes, I gave it— Oh. I get it." That was why she came back. "Thanks, man."

"No problem."

"I gotta go."

"Go."

Riley hit disconnect.

He moved close to her, putting his head on the pillow to whisper in her ear. "How can I make it work? What do you need me to say?"

She took his hand, holding it in front of her face, studying his palm. "Darci gave me half of Colborn. Wait, it's half of her half."

It struck Riley as an odd move for Darci to make. "Why?"

"Apparently, it should have belonged to my dad. I really am one of them, Riley. It's more than just being Darci's sister."

That was interesting. But Riley didn't want to talk about their families anymore.

He cut to the chase. "I love you, Kalissa."

She shifted to face him, her features close up and crystal clear. "I figured you must."

He chuckled gently and smoothed her hair, brushed her ear, stroked her cheek, then he kissed her lips.

"Shane told me you turned down his offer," she said.

"I only want you."

"I think it was a test. I think he did it for me. So I'd know for sure."

"Shane's pretty shrewd that way."

She gathered his hand and drew it to her chest. "I love you, Riley."

"Oh, sweetheart."

"I missed you so much."

"You don't have to miss me anymore. I wish I had a ring. I

wish we had champagne. It would be better if we were dressed. This isn't the kind of story you can tell the grandchildren."

"We can do all that later," said Kalissa.

"Marry me," said Riley.

"Yes. Oh, yes."

* * * * *

If you loved this CHICAGO SONS *novel
by Barbara Dunlop pick up the first book
in the series about men who work hard,
love harder and live with their fathers' legacies…*

SEX, LIES AND THE CEO

Available now from Harlequin Desire!

*If you're on Twitter, tell us what you think of
Harlequin Desire! #harlequindesire*